BIRD IN THE NET

Also by Frank Parrish

FIRE IN THE BARLEY

SNARE IN THE DARK

STING OF THE HONEYBEE

BAIT ON THE HOOK

DEATH IN THE RAIN

FLY IN THE COBWEB

Frank Parrish

BIRD

IN THE NET

HARPER & ROW, PUBLISHERS, New York
Cambridge, Philadelphia, San Francisco, Washington
London, Mexico City, São Paulo, Singapore, Sydney

This book was published in England under the title *Caught in the Birdlime*.

FIRST U.S. EDITION 1988

ISBN: 0-06-015879-4

LIBRARY OF CONGRESS CATALOG CARD NUMBER: 87-45760

88 89 90 91 92 HC 10 9 8 7 6 5 4 3 2 1

I

Dusk, early October, the candles glowing from the altar in the Church of All Saints, Medwell Fratrorum. It was a Service of Induction of a new Incumbent. The Suffragan Bishop of Milchester – the square-cut stone of his episcopal ring giving back the candle-light as he gestured widely in wide white sleeves – asked the people of the parishes of Medwell Fratrorum, Medwell Zelston and Winterbourne Thrumpton to make welcome their new Shepherd and his family, to ask them to their homes – not to wait to be visited, but to take the initiative in this new relationship.

Dan Mallett, not a regular church-goer, thought he would not ask the new Vicar into his home. For the Vicar and his wife, together with Dan and his mother, there would scarcely be room. It was true that Dan took up little space, being a small, wiry man, easily overlooked; but Dan's mother, though smaller still, seemed by the force of her resentful personality to occupy ten times as much space as she physically displaced; and it was evident that the Vicar's pretty young wife was about to have a baby.

Dan, perched at the end of a pew right at the back of the church, was wearing his best dark banker's suit, uniform of the days of his peonage. He had tried to get out of the cottage without his mother seeing him in this finery. It only reminded her of what might have been, of her dreams for him, of her dreams for her own respectable and middle-class old age. It only turned knives in a wound that would never close. It only put her in a rage, and spoiled her appetite. (It did not spoil Dan's appetite – nothing ever did.)

The old Vicar had been the Old Vicar, his actual name virtually forgotten, who had been apathetically liked, by and large, and of whose sermons no one had ever understood a word. His wife had been better known and less liked, being a toffee-nosed bossy-boots who tried to interfere with the way the village brought up its children. She had never had children of her own – what did she know about it? She presided over various Groups, whose meetings were announced by the Vicar among the Notices and Banns of Marriage during Matins. Few people attended the Groups; most who did were pensioners with nothing else to do. The Old Vicar and his wife did not seem to have a happy marriage, or an unhappy marriage; they did not seem to have a marriage at all.

It was not so with the new Vicar and his wife. Though physically separated during the Service of Induction by the requirements of ritual, they looked as married as anybody should. He looked a cheerful fellow, maybe nearing forty; she looked a nice person, maybe nearing thirty. Seemingly the child was their first. The village was in a mood to welcome them, although the arrival of a new Vicar was not nearly as important an event as would have been the arrival of a new postmaster, grocer, or licensee of the Chestnut Horse.

Dan Mallett's presence at the Service of Induction went largely unnoticed, because he was small and he sat at the back. Those members of the congregation who saw him assumed he had come to nick the collection money or the altar candlesticks. They were surprised to see him, and could only explain it on such grounds. Dan was himself surprised to be there. He would not have stolen the collection, nor the church silver, even to help pay for his mother's hip operation: nor would he have felt comfortable about pinching anything from a house whose owners were in church. He would not have found it easy to explain this scruple, which nobody else would have believed – not Jim Gundry the village policeman, nor any local game-keeper. Not Dan's own mother. Least of all her. She *had* seen him go out, though he tried to get clear like a mouse through a knot-hole. There was very little she missed. Her pins were unsteady, but her eyes and her brain seemed to grow sharper with the years. She was, of course, too proud to remark on his best suit, which he hated and which he wore only for the most compelling reasons.

She simply said, 'Ye ben boozen, wenchen or thieven.'

6

It was not a question, but a catalogue of the things which would get a little villain like Dan out of the house on an October evening.

'Be about an hour,' said Dan, wasting one of his smiles on her unforgiving face.

He went through the door with a kind of smirking apology in his walk, and bicycled to the lych-gate opposite the Chestnut Horse.

The reason Dan was in church was the reason he had, over the years, done many unprofitable and time-consuming things. It was a girl. She was a newcomer to the village, daughter of a near-nob called Captain Muspratt. Dan had on occasion adopted the identity of a Captain*, and he thought Captain Muspratt was no more like a real Captain than he himself was; and Dan reckoned he was as unlike a Captain as anybody he ever heard of. All this was terribly unimportant when you got a good look at Fiona Muspratt. Dan had had a good look at her when she was swimming, in a small one-piece, in the Barclays' pool at the end of August.

It was a new pool in an old garden, and the Barclays were new people in an old house. The house was Court Farm, on the edge of Winterbourne Thrumpton, so called because it was neither a court nor a farm. It had been the farmhouse of a Court which no longer existed; the farm no longer existed, either, except as vestigial paddocks on the edge of a small council estate. Terence Barclay was not (as far as Lady Simpson knew, talking about the matter in quite an undignified way to Dan) a member of the famous banking or brewing families of his name; but by the standards of the area he was certainly rich – in a class with Sir George Simpson. He was just the sort of semi-retired near-nob from whom Dan derived the visible part of his earnings. He went to London for a night or two, two or three times a month. He had a roguish moustache and a red silk scarf. He spoke banteringly to the girls in the post office, chaffing them about their love-lives. Dan guessed it was his idea, not Monica Barclay's, to ask Fiona Muspratt to swim. He was certainly very

---

* A deplorable example of this imposture is recorded in *Bait on the Hook*, by the same author.

attentive to her, watching her closely in case she drowned. He could hardly be blamed for that: Dan was watching her closely too.

Dan was not swimming in the pool but clipping a hedge. He was dressed at the opposite end of his personal spectrum from the Captain he sometimes impersonated – he was being a professional yokel. What it took was old, old corduroy trousers tied below the knee with binder-twine, and a cap and a mole-skin waistcoat several sizes too large. He put a wisp of hay in his hair when he arrived at the Barclays', but he took it out again, as being overacting. He might as well have left it in. The whole role was absurdly overacted. He was aware of this, but people like the Barclays never seemed to mind. It made his wages higher and his work less.

Unfortunately it distanced him, on that occasion, and some others, from the likes of Fiona Muspratt. You could be a rural fossil, fount of quirky homespun philosophy, or you could make a pass at a pretty girl who was being entertained by nobs. To try both at the same time was to court humiliation – Dan had tried, and he knew. But he could easily find out all that anybody knew about the girl, from the Barclays and in the bar of the Chestnut Horse. She was well educated. On top of that she was a shorthand typist. She worked for an estate agent in Milchester, to which she drove herself daily in her own little Renault. She was musical. She had been asked to join the church choir almost as soon as the Muspratts moved in to Cobbett's Cottage. She liked swimming and tennis, and prob-ably many other things which the oracles of the Chestnut Horse could only guess at.

She had a marvellous figure, which like her tastes could only be guessed at as she sat in a purple surplice in the choir-stall, but which Dan had examined, between twigs of hornbeam, on the edge of the Barclays' pool.

Dan properly met her two weekends later. She was coming out of the post office as he was going in. She was not the only reason for his going in, but she was the reason for his going in when he did. He held the door for her. She was laden with bags of shopping, since the post office sold many things besides stamps. It was the weekend shopping for the Muspratt family, and Dan contrived, by means of officious helpfulness, to knock some of it out of her arms. Potatoes rolled about the village street. Dan and the girl had a merry time of it, chasing errant main-crop potatoes. She was wearing a blue cotton dress; she had sandals on her feet and her legs were bare. Her hair was light brown and wavy, her eyes grey, her nose small, her mouth a little wide. She was just the sort of girl Dan liked, though it was true that he also liked blondes, redheads, and sultry sirens with raven hair.

Dan was dressed in in-between clothes that left most of his options open – tan-coloured pants, an open-necked shirt, as worn for mowing a lawn by the Assistant Bank Manager he might by now have been.

Fiona was in a mood to be receptive to wide, guileless blue eyes, to a smile as broad as her own in a wedge-shaped, weatherbeaten face. Without disloyalty to her parents, she found weekends in Medwell a bit boring. There seemed to be nobody of her age, and it would have been difficult to entertain them if they had existed. The people who had asked her to things were older.

The small brown man who helped her to chase potatoes was older, too, but not much older. His smile had the quality of making you smile back. His eyes were a remarkable colour, as he had no doubt often been told.

'All present and correct, I think,' he said, piling recaptured potatoes into the back of her Renault.

'Thank you very much,' said Fiona.

'No more than my duty,' said Dan, 'as I caused the disaster. I did it on purpose, actually.'

'What? Why? What do you mean?'

'Couldn't bear to be a ship that passed in the night,' said Dan. 'Couldn't endure the idea.'

'But you live somewhere near here?'

'Tolerably handy.'

'Where?'

'A sort of cranny in the bark of an old tree. You can only tell it's a house if someone explains to you.'

'Did you really make me drop those potatoes on purpose?'

'Speaking of potatoes,' said Dan, 'if you bake them in the

back-end of a bonfire, and eat them with sour cream and chives –'

'We weren't speaking of potatoes. I was asking you if you really –'

'Or putting it another way, will you do me the honour of dining with me?'

Dan had not used these words, or any remotely like them, since his days in the bank. He was completely astonished by them, as, evidently, was the girl.

'But we don't know each other,' said the girl. This seemed to Dan a comment, a valid point, perhaps an objection, but not a refusal.

'We're putting that right by the minute,' said Dan. 'The feast of reason and the flow of soul. Allow me to present myself. Dan Mallett, at your service.'

The girl stared at him in blank disbelief.

'You can't be,' she said.

Dan understood. The Barclays, and probably others, had told the Muspratts about Dan. He knew that, inconspicuous as he tried to be, he did get talked about. He was locally famous (if you took the view of the nobs who employed him) or, putting it another way, notorious (if you took the view of gamekeepers who tried to protect their pheasant-poults). Jim Gundry the policeman, who talked about Dan more than most, said he was the biggest villain unhung. Fiona Muspratt might easily have heard that, too. None of it added up to an Assistant Bank Manager dressed for mowing his own lawn on a hot September Saturday.

''Ere ben two on I, seemenly,' said Dan, in his broadest and most treacly parody of antique rural Wessex. 'Tes confusen.'

''Taint,' said the girl unexpectedly, and suddenly roared with laughter.

That was the moment when Dan, laughing, really fell for her.

She said she would have dinner with him if he would come to church. They shook hands on this curious bargain, unlike any Dan had ever made. Dan allowed himself his lecherous smile, eighty per cent candlepower.

He held the car door for her as she slid in under the wheel.

The movement pushed her skimpy cotton skirt up her bare thighs.

'Don't peek,' said Fiona. 'But of course you've seen me swimming.'

The Barclays *had* talked about him. Probably they had pointed him out, as a rare specimen not to be found in every garden. The girl was forewarned. She saw through him. She called all his bluffs. It was unnerving but refreshing. His ambition as regards Fiona, already clearly defined, was probably unattainable. Certainly it would be hard work. A girl who laughed as this one laughed was worth any amount of hard work.

It was worth putting on his best dark suit, and exciting the fury of his mother, and sitting in a pew at the back of the church during the Service of Induction of a new Incumbent.

Fiona Muspratt, during the sermon, looked for Dan in the congregation without seeming to do so. She should not have been looking for small men with blue eyes during Divine Service, but attending to the words of the Bishop. She did not feel very guilty. She thought the God to whom they were singing hymns and psalms would understand that, in putting somebody like Dan Mallett into the world, He would cause young ladies in choir-stalls to look for them in the congregation.

She thought she glimpsed him right at the back, but it was impossible to be sure without craning her neck. She could not behave so improperly, new to the village as she was, with the Simpsons and the Calloways and so forth filling the front pews. There behind the Calloways was Terence Barclay, by himself. That was odd, thought Fiona irreverently – you'd think she'd come to church and he'd stay away. She suffered from migraines. He'd got away on his own, as apparently he often did, though this time only to church. He was an old pest, a bit pathetic in being both old and a pest, and Fiona tried with moderate success to feel charitable about him. He had tried to peek when she was changing in the hut beside their pool, and he couldn't keep his freckled old hands to himself. Fiona would never go swimming in that pool again, except as one of a large party. Still, it would not do to be seen searching the congregation, by him or any of the others, by any of the people her parents were getting to know. She did not want to reveal to Dan, supposing he was there, that she cared whether he was there or not.

The thought of having dinner with Dan filled her with amusement. It was something to look forward to, but only if he had kept his side of the bargain.

Sandra Hedges, wife of the Reverend Gordon Hedges, was also looking at the congregation. She could hardly fail to do so, since she was in the front pew of the shallow transept, where the pews faced inwards at the nave. She was almost under the pulpit, from which the Bishop was making friendly and encouraging noises. Sandra was looking at her new neighbours, the people amongst whom she and Gordon would be living and working.

They looked like people, just people dressed up for church – like British people, not quite like her own people in a very small town near Kearney, Nebraska. They would like Gordon, because everybody did. They might find it surprising to have an American parson's wife, but once they had got over that she thought she might get along with them. She got along with most people – with everybody, really, one particular poisonous individual excepted, and that was a long way away and a long time ago.

Sandra was happy beyond anything that had seemed possible.

She had run away to Europe with every penny that disaster had left her. With the dollar strong against European currencies, she managed pretty well for a surprisingly long time. People were endlessly kind, and she could travel pretty rough. She was seldom alone and never lonely. By the time she made it to England she was running short of money, and her conscience was telling her to get back to work. It would be difficult to get a work permit in any European country where she might want to settle, so work meant America. She shrank from going home. As soon as she stepped off the airplane she would be vulnerable.

Sooner or later they would find her and drag her back, and it would be worse because she had run away.

In London she came across a party she had met in Rome, a thing which was always happening. They were younger than herself, students, serious, travelling at her economical level; moving with that group was nothing but a pleasure, because they taught her so much about architecture and she could teach them a little about history. They somehow got hold of a little bus, and they toured around looking at cathedrals and castles, and staying at bed-and-breakfast places.

They went to Winchester and to Salisbury. They were all Episcopalians, and they went to services in those great churches. Sandra had been raised a Baptist, but life had turned her into an atheist. In front of the choir-screen in Winchester Cathedral she felt herself turning back again.

In Salisbury they went to a concert, something to do with the cathedral. In the interval of the concert there was wine to be bought by the glass. Sandra drank very little – she had drunk very little in her life – but wine was another thing her young friends were enthusiastic about. The white wine at the concert was very cold. It was expensive, but they bought it because they were supporting various charities by doing so.

There were quite a lot of clergy at the concert, naturally enough since it was being held in a cathedral close. One of Sandra's group got talking to one of the Reverends, who was also drinking wine in the interval. They talked about the music, which was Renaissance and baroque and magnificent. The young Americans introduced themselves, and introduced Sandra. It was the most accidental thing in the world, but as Gordon afterwards said not so totally accidental, since they were people who came to that sort of concert in that sort of place.

He was ten years older than herself, Sandra thought. He was six foot and something, and looked like an athlete. He was sunburned, and his hair was unruly. He wore a clerical collar and a lightweight suit. His voice was as English as the spire of Salisbury Cathedral in the Constable painting. Sandra concluded afterwards, with a sense of joyful shock, that she had fallen in love with him that first evening, right there by the table where they were selling over-chilled wine.

He was with friends, but not with a wife and not with a girl. It came out in the conversation that he was not married, although his Bishop wanted him to be. It just came out, by way of something somebody said; Sandra had wanted to know, but of course she had not asked.

And then they met again, coming away at the end. Sandra felt her heart lift when she saw that unruly brown hair. It seemed like another miraculous chance. Gordon said afterwards that it wasn't chance at all – that he had struggled like a madman through the crowd to meet them 'by chance' at the exit.

Sandra's friends had to get back to their studies. Sandra stayed. Gordon found her a cheap, decent place to live. He was teaching in the city. She met his friends, and when some of his family came to see him, she met them, too.

They found they were eating together, often noon and evening, most days of the week. They went to concerts, films, exhibitions together; they went for huge walks, sandwiches in their pockets, and drank beer outside little pubs in the evening sun.

They discussed everything. They discussed religion. It was obviously important to Gordon to know just where Sandra stood, even if he had to be a little impertinent about it. She said she stood exactly where he stood, wherever that was, and always would. She just about came out and proposed to him.

His family, who lived in Somerset, were as welcoming as they could be. His father was a doctor, nearing retirement; his mother was as active as a terrier, particularly among the weeds in the herbaceous border; his brother was a Lieutenant-Commander in the Navy, married to a girl from Scotland; his sister, who lived nearby, was married to a veterinarian. They all went to church together in the Somerset village. The Church of England service meant more and more to Sandra, because of the beauty of the language and of the buildings, because it was Gordon's. She was instructed by a friend of Gordon's, and received into the Church of England. She was confirmed in Salisbury Cathedral, one of two or three adults and scores of schoolchildren.

The Bishop was very kind to her at the tea-party after the Confirmation. He said he admired Gordon's taste and envied his luck. All Gordon's family kissed Sandra, and pretended not to notice when she burst into tears.

It was after that miraculous occasion that Gordon's mother told Sandra about Gordon's money. Gordon had never mentioned it. It was not such a very large amount, but it was enough to make a very large difference to a country parson. It derived from a godmother who had latterly lived in South Africa. The rest of the family was thankful and unenvious – they were all paid more than Gordon would ever be. Sandra was not to expect a lot of luxuries, but she could rely on financial security. Unlike parsons who depended entirely on their stipends, Gordon could afford such things as health insurance, private music lessons for his children, durable furniture.

The engagement was announced in the newspapers, and the Banns were read. These events were of gigantic importance to Sandra and Gordon, of some importance to his family and closest friends, and of no importance to anybody else at all. Still, they established Sandra as a speck in the fabric of the establishment, a person with a local habitation and a name, somebody who was not hiding, who could easily be found, who was now recognised and greeted by a large and ever-growing circle of acquaintances. It was not a surprise that the American journalist found her, although it was a great surprise that she should want to do so.

The journalist was called Andrea Kling, a New York girl working for a national women's magazine. She was on a kind of working vacation. She had picked up a newspaper in a train, read the engagement announcement, and wondered idly how a girl from Nebraska came to be getting married to a Church of England parson in Salisbury Cathedral. She thought there might be a nice, warm-hearted little story in it, and she found there was. Gordon and Sandra were photographed in the cathedral close. The journalist talked more than she listened, but she seemed a nice person. They sent Sandra a copy of the magazine when the story was printed. A few of the facts had got a little bent, but the writer was almost too kind about them all – Gordon's deep Christian faith and his rumpled hair, Sandra's long legs and the hint of freckles on her forehead, the roses in Gordon's mother's garden. And the couple had met in such cultured and romantic circumstances! And the bride had been received into her sweetheart's church, and a Bishop had laid hands on her head! Gordon's mother had the article photocopied, and the Bishop laughed at the description of himself.

One of the things that got a little bent was the size of Gordon's fortune. The magazine did not give a figure, but it did give an impression, and the impression was exaggerated. Only Gordon's mother could have been the source. She would not have talked about it in any spirit of boasting, but so that Andrea Kling would not go away feeling sorry for Sandra and Gordon, thinking that they were embarking on married life on such a tiny salary. Gordon's mother was far too good-hearted and trusting to be discreet.

There was one small, itching particle of worry in Sandra's mind. She wondered how widely the magazine circulated in remote parts of Middle America. She wondered if it reached small towns near Kearney, Nebraska. She could not share her worry, even with Gordon. And it was only a tiny worry, because she felt supremely safe. She was surrounded and protected by millions of British, who if they wished her anything wished her well. She was walled by the ancient stones of the Church of England. Most powerful of all, she had Gordon's arm around her. She was the safest person she ever heard of.

They were married, by the Bishop, in the Choir of the Cathedral. On Sandra's side there was nobody at all, and she was given away by the bridegroom's brother. She had told them all that she had no blood-relations that she knew of, and it was for all practical purposes the truth. She was orphaned and kinless, and she had been friendless. Never again. Now she was part of a family and she had hundreds of friends. The Bishop said as much in his Address, smiling at Sandra. She smiled back, involuntarily, through her veil.

They honeymooned in Pembrokeshire, on a coast with fantastic rock formations and a sky teeming with birds. It went without saying that Gordon had hitherto been strictly chaste; if Sandra had had any experience, she did not wound her husband

16

by talking about it. They had a tentative night or two, then all came right. It was a revelation to them both.

'D'you know, I never really realised,' murmured Gordon in the happy small hours, 'quite how much God had given us. That's a cathedral and a Titian and a symphony rolled up into one.'

'And a sunset and this coastline and a swim by moonlight,' said Sandra sleepily.

In the next few days they smiled whenever they caught one another's eyes. They thought their overwhelming happiness must show in their faces, and they were right.

They came back to Gordon's appointment, to be taken up the following year, to the living of Medwell Fratrorum, with its two tiny daughter parishes.

They spent Christmas with Gordon's family, the happiest Christmas Sandra had ever spent, the first happy Christmas she had ever spent.

The baby was conceived on a magical night in February. When it was born it would have a home. It would be born to the life of the Vicarage in Medwell Fratrorum.

Photographic slides of the intervening months of ever-growing happiness blinked on and off in Sandra's mind as she sat through the Service of Induction. Her own pregnancy underlay it all, like a sward of joy. Below that lay the nourishing soil of her religious faith, which had been there all along without her knowing it. And below that again was bedrock: Gordon: her love for Gordon and his love for her. To meet absolute goodness was remarkable; to live with it was an hourly-renewed miracle. Sandra could understand that saints could laugh loud and long, and be wonderful lovers, and have a half-guilty passion for raspberries and cream. Gordon was security and inspiration and fun.

Idly, her mind divided between her own thoughts and the progress of the ancient service, she looked at her new neighbours. People, British people, her adopted tribe. Faces still showing traces of the late-summer sun. Hair neat (all but Gordon's, which nothing would ever make neat), collars and ties, dark suits or tweeds, the older women in hats – people not individually remarkable in any way, but collectively not to be mistaken for those of any other country. Sandra wondered at feeling so completely at home when she was transplanted from five thousand miles away.

Thick grey hair, thin ginger hair, copious curls, a severe little knot at the back of the neck, twin-sets, light overcoats, a few pearls.

There were some familiar faces, people met over tea or sherry. There were faces beginning to be well known, several cups of tea, several glasses of sherry.

There were Sir George and Lady Simpson. He was the first British knight Sandra had ever got to know, and he seemed like anybody else. There were Mr and Mrs Calloway, of whom Sandra felt a slight, guilty and indefinable suspicion – their garden was like Sandra's mother-in-law's garden, but more so, ten times more so, too much so – there was something dubious about people who had real flowers that looked like plastic. The Calloways were real people, but to Sandra they looked like plastic.

Behind the Calloways Sandra could see Terence Barclay, from whom she also fought a little shy, for more explicable reasons. She was sure he would have made a pass at her if she had not been heavily pregnant when they met. He was handsome in that kind of elderly way, with a jaunty grey moustache and polished hair: he looked like an advertisement in an American magazine for some specifically British product (tonic water or a raincoat): like Uncle Fred in the Wodehouse books, forever twirling his moustache and looking at girls' legs. His wife had an air of having put up with it for twenty-five years, and of being prepared to go on putting up with it. She was not visible. Terence Barclay had left her at home. Sandra checked herself from speculating whether that was his choice or hers.

Across the aisle were Admiral Jenkyn and his wife, an elderly couple too, he long retired, who lived in a house by the river three hundred yards from the church, the lawn stretching to the waterside and the kitchen garden to the village cricket ground. The Admiral was Chairman of the Parochial Church Council. This was one reason why Gordon and Sandra were staying with them until they moved into the Vicarage; another was that the Jenkyns had plenty of room and apparently plenty of money.

18

The Vicarage. Sandra's thoughts strayed to what would soon be her home. It was a smallish, newish house in the village street, where it belonged, a hundred yards from the church in the other direction. The Diocesan Finance Committee had sold the old Vicarage, which was expensive to heat and had a four-acre garden, and bought this decent little dwelling to house the Hedges. It had a quarter-acre garden and solid-fuel heating; it was light and airy and the windows fitted; it would be the place to which the villages and the countryside would bring their troubles.

Would they? What troubles? The faces Sandra could see did not look as though they had any troubles. Some were sun-browned, some pale, some serious, some sleepy, none neurotic or tortured or racked by anything worse than a twinge of rheumatism.

Sandra felt not like a missionary, but like someone coming to a tranquil and welcoming home.

Kind faces, stolid faces, alert faces, bored faces, some amusing faces.

A face which was distinctive. Not bizarre, but somehow exotic. Prematurely silver hair, thick and glossy, brushed straight back. The face handsome but a little fleshy, the nose a little thick, the flesh sagging below the chin. A coat like a kind of tartan, made of some thin material. It was an un-English coat; it was an un-English face.

Sandra recognised the face. After a moment of utter disbelief, she had to accept the blankly incredible. She felt physically sick and very frightened.

2

Fiona Muspratt lost hope of identifying Dan. She went on trying, but without hope. When the choir and congregation were sitting, there was a limit to the searching she could do; when the choir was standing, the congregation was standing too, and if Dan was at the back he would be hidden by larger persons in front of him. Nearly everybody in church was larger than Dan.

Sitting in her choir-stall, Fiona looked straight across the Sanctuary at the opposite choir-stalls, and at the men and women and children who sat there in purple surplices looking as though butter wouldn't melt in their mouths. By moving her eyes a little to the left, Fiona could see the people in the front pew of the transept, facing the nave, and the people in the front few pews of the nave, facing the altar. There was nobody there she much wanted to see, except the new Vicar's wife. Fiona had not met her, although many people in the parish already had. Fiona wanted to meet her. She looked great. She was very good-looking, in what Fiona thought was a specifically American kind of way – a Farah Fawcett way – strong features, lovely hair, healthy teeth. There was a hint of freckles across her forehead, which Fiona also had. Her baby looked pretty imminent. The great thing about her was that she looked so happy. She looked happy to be in this church, among these people, married to this parson. To Fiona, her happiness was so evident that it was happy-making. A lot of things were wrong with the world, but the Reverend and Mrs Gordon Hedges were among the things that were right with the world.

Something entirely extraordinary happened, something in-explicable and shocking. A twinge of acute pain? A demon suddenly materialising? Mrs Hedges' face, her whole visible personality, went in a blink from happiness to abject misery. It was as though she had been shot from the comforting ritual, the cheerful welcome, of this church into a desert with hideous silhouettes against a colourless sky: as though the husband she loved was being tortured, or branded as a sadistic pervert. It was as violent as that. It was a different person sitting there. It was a haggard, ageing woman with a wasting disease. It was naked misery. It was terror.

Under Fiona's eyes, Mrs Hedges got a grip of herself. Her face now showed nothing. If it did not show the radiant happiness of ten seconds before, it did not show the anguish of five seconds before. The changes were so rapid that probably nobody else in the congregation had seen anything. Fiona herself was facing Mrs Hedges, and had, by chance, been looking directly at her. Otherwise she would not have seen what had happened. She wished she had not.

Dan Mallett saw Fiona Muspratt trying to locate him. At least, she was trying to locate somebody in the congregation, and he hoped it was him. The reason for that, he told himself, would simply be their bargain. If she saw him, she would know he was there; if not, she would have to take his word for it. From the things he knew she had heard, she might not be quite ready to do that, not if he couldn't produce an independent witness or two.

He could produce independent witnesses, but the scene did not play itself. 'Yes, we saw Dan Mallett in church, obviously bent on nicking the candlesticks.'

It would be better if some event occurred which he could only know about by having been there. 'I can prove I was there, because after the second hymn Mr Calloway's false teeth fell out. I couldn't know that unless I'd seen it, so where would you like to have dinner?'

That would be fine, only, as the service majestically progressed, nothing like that happened.

And then something extraordinary did happen. It happened so quickly that Dan was not quite sure afterwards if he had really seen it. He knew, unfortunately, that he had seen it.

He had been looking with keen pleasure at Fiona Muspratt, in profile except when she was looking for him, candle-lit, looking rather solemn and absolutely sweet. The thoughts that the sight of her engendered were totally unsuitable for a Service of Induction. He looked away with an effort, to the front pew of the transept. It was worth a look, because the new Vicar's wife, young Mrs Hedges, was sitting there. He could see the new Vicar, too, in one of the throne-like oak chairs below the choir-stalls. For all the openness and friendliness of his face, the Vicar looked a difficult bloke to con. He might be amused by Dan's *Under the Greenwood Tree* act – he looked a man who would laugh readily: he had those kinds of lines around his eyes – but he would not be lured under its spell. He would probably dig his own garden anyway, and put up his own shelves. He would probably do these things a lot quicker than Dan was accustomed to doing them, the welcome end of one job being the unwelcome beginning of another. As for Mrs Hedges, Dan found that he didn't even want to try to con her. You met people like that sometimes – a sort of light flashed and a voice said 'Hands off.' It was quite inconvenient sometimes, quite annoying, a series of chances missed.

Nothing would have induced him, for example, to nick anything from anybody involved with the previous year's Medwell Symposium of the Performing Arts,* because those people had become his friends. They made what might have appeared the ludicrous mistake of trusting him, and their trust had had the effect, as though chemical, of making him trustworthy. With Mrs Hedges he would be trustworthy, supposing they had any contact at all, because nobody could nick anything from anybody who looked so happy.

Dan accused himself of sentimentality, and found himself guilty.

It was at this point of his thoughts – a long, long way from the service – that the oddity occurred. It took very few seconds, and it was in one place only. It was in Mrs Hedges' face. Off that attractive face was wiped, as though by a blade, the expression

* Dan's adventures among these eccentrics are recounted in *Fly in the Cobweb*, by the same author.

of happiness. On to it was spread, as though by a high-pressure pump, an expression of bottomless misery, so devasting that it was impossible to guess if it were caused by physical pain or what. That too disappeared, leaving nothing behind – no expression at all. It was obvious to Dan that Mrs Hedges was exercising gigantic self-control. He admired her, but it was distressing and embarrassing to watch. He looked away. He looked at Fiona. He saw that Fiona was looking at Mrs Hedges, and he saw that she had seen what he had seen. Her face showed worry, compassion, puzzlement.

She was a really nice girl, and she was unhappy at somebody's unhappiness.

Sandra Hedges got her face under control, but not her thoughts.

She tried to plug the hole in the dyke against the flood of hateful memories, but they engulfed her.

Her first memories were of the early 1960s, when she lived with her mother and father in a little house, made apparently of cardboard, at the edge of town. She was an only child, but whether by accident or design she never knew. It was not the sort of question that could be asked. If there were jobs in town, her father didn't get them. People said there were a lot of jobs in defence and aerospace and such in Southern California, in places like San Diego. Sandra's father went away over the Rockies to get one of these fat jobs. He would send them money, and they would join him in a few weeks. They never heard from him again. He climbed on the Greyhound bus one Tuesday morning, and hummed away out of their lives. They never knew if he was alive, dead, rich, married again, or what.

Sandra's mother went to work, and the job killed her. The job was in a little ice-cream factory, ununionised, uninspected as far as anybody knew; she got pneumonia and died very quickly without any fuss. Still a little girl, Sandra went to a married cousin of her mother's. They were childless; they had a farm; they were rigidly conventional, fanatical about appearances, teetotal and non-smoking; they worked hard and they worked Sandra hard. It was their duty to take in Sandra, and they took her in. It was their duty to make her fight the never-ending battle against Satan, and they did that too.

They had inherited a lot of books, from some other kin who liked books. They were proud of the look of book-lined shelves, and pointed them out to people. A wall of books was rare in that kind of house, in that part of the state. They did not read the books, but Sandra did, any moment that schoolwork and chores permitted.

That was how she was able to get her diploma, and how she came to be Assistant Librarian in the town's public library, and how she came to meet Harry Curtis.

Harry was on the road (soft furnishings) and the town was in his territory. There was only one store which handled his line of goods – materials for drapes, chair-covers, tablecloths – and in the ordinary way, he told her, he visited no more than twice a year. But he made bends and zigzags in his route, so that he visited the town almost every week, and then almost every day. He dropped around to the library; he took Sandra to Delmonico's and the Rainbow Bar. People began to talk. Travelling salesmen were a proverbial hazard, figuring in most of the stories men told one another in washrooms.

Sandra's adoptive family forbade her to see Harry again, which had the predictable effect. She was a stifled twenty-two-year-old, being treated like a delinquent teenager. She had to meet Harry in secret, which she did.

He was handsome, big and strong and beautiful. His hair was prematurely grey, which made him not less attractive but more so. She was terribly flattered to be chosen by such a sophisticated, travelled, handsome older man. Not so very much older, but full of worldly wisdom and wisecracks and a cynical view of life which delighted her. She had met it in books. She felt delightfully wicked, listening to his contemptuous opinions of Primitive Baptist communities like hers; she felt sinful and elated when he kissed her, when she felt his hands on her body and his tongue on hers. She came alive, trembling, ardently responding. It was all completely new to her and she liked it very much. She had, to be sure, met the same kind of thing in books.

A letter came from a lawyer in La Jolla, taking a long time to reach her because she was living in a different house. Her father had been killed in some kind of industrial accident, and there was a girl who knew that Sandra and her mother existed, and where they were. Sandra was left nearly eight thousand dollars. She offered some to her adoptive family, to pay them back for all they had spent on her over the years. They refused; they said she had worked her way; they said she deserved a change of luck. Sandra would have changed her view of them, out of gratitude, but they continued to forbid her ever to see Harry again.

Somebody saw Sandra and Harry, in his car on a road outside of town. Sandra was too old to whip, but only just; she was not too old to be locked in. She escaped over the roof of an outhouse, and ran away with Harry.

A Justice of the Peace married them, away in Omaha.

Harry made her drunk, and the marriage was consummated between bouts of her throwing up. What she afterwards remembered was the throwing up.

It was three days before she discovered that Harry had lost his job. He had fiddled his records and his travels, invented sales, left important customers unvisited. He said it was all on her account, all for love of her. She could go on believing this for a month; after two months she stopped believing in anything. He showed no signs of trying to get another job. He did not get her drunk again, but he went away on his own and got himself drunk. Pretty soon she realised that when her eight thousand was gone, Harry would be gone.

She ran away from him, back to what had been her home, back to her adoptive parents. They would not take her in. She turned away, in tears, from the door that had been slammed in her face, and there was Harry. She still had some money, and he had chased it and caught it. That was the first time he seriously beat her. She ran away two more times, and he caught her, and those were two more times he seriously beat her.

It seemed that Harry Curtis was not his real name.

She rediscovered belief in evil, but not belief in God.

She thought about suicide, often and often, but she was damned if she was going to enrich Harry by getting out of his way.

She tried one more appeal to her adoptive parents. They did not turn her away because they had gone away. Somebody else was living at the farm. Nobody knew where they had gone, or if they knew they would not tell Sandra. Harry found her and caught her and beat her up, and spent some more of her money.

Sandra had supposed that Harry was as alone in the world as she was. No kin, he had told her, no folks to be bothering the two of them. He had told her that when she still believed what he said. She stopped believing anything that he said, but she carried on supposing that he had no kin. It was another lie. He told her so himself, not caring that he was exposing himself as a liar, not giving a damn what she thought about anything. There was a girl called Cora, not much older than Sandra, fluffy, like a girl on the top of an old-fashioned box of candy, very blonde, surprisingly a trained nurse, surprisingly Harry's cousin. Sandra never met her, but Harry had a big photograph of her, expensively framed but kept in a drawer with his fancy socks and his gun. When Harry went out to get drunk on Sandra's money, he was not always alone or with roadhouse drummers and drabs; sometimes, he said, he met Cora. He said he would not make Sandra acquainted with Cora, because Cora was too superior. He boasted about his bright baby cousin, the trained nurse, the professional lady. He called her the Peach of Nebraska. Sometimes he said he loved her. He said she was far above him, far too good for him. Maybe this was a casual cruelty, said only to hurt Sandra. Maybe it was true.

Sandra spent weeks preparing an escape which she decided would be her last. If she didn't get away this time, she would end it all, leaving the remnants of her money where Harry couldn't get it. She went by the most devious routes to New York, and on to Paris. Her chin was on her shoulder every inch of the way – she expected Harry in every train and bus and airplane, in every room she went into, round every corner.

Harry would have been very angry, being cheated of her money. He would have been thirsty. He would have been forced into getting another job, or into stealing or mugging.

He must have seen the magazine, with her picture, with Gordon's name, with the names of Salisbury and of Medwell Fratrorum. The magazine gave dates. Sandra wondered how Harry had raised the money to come to England, and where he was living, and on what.

In the weeks after her escape, when she was darting from bolt-hole to bolt-hole, covering her tracks, getting her money to New York, getting a passport, she had asked herself again and again why she had rushed on self-destruction. Harry was such an obvious fraud and layabout and bully. Everybody had seen this, except her. Everybody had been instantly certain and absolutely right. The answers were pretty obvious – her innocence and inexperience, his skill in flattery and love-making, the repressive bleakness of her home, all the usual things. Sandra had been depressed by how usual her story was – her disaster was second-hand stuff, a many-times-told tale, an old chestnut, familiar to the Victorians. Europe had enabled her to put the whole thing behind her. She felt safe. Like many well-read Americans, she felt at home in Europe – she felt that she was greeting the Mona Lisa and Michelangelo's David and Salisbury Cathedral as old friends.

Harry became a bad dream, hardly remembered in the morning. The time with him was a blank, the tape wiped.

The congregation stood. Like an automaton Sandra stood. Everybody knelt. She knelt. She tried to pray. Her mind was too confused to form words of prayer, and when she found words of supplication a black oak door blocked them from getting to God.

When the prayer ended, the congregation stood. The people stood not all at once but a little raggedly, many uncertain, in this rarely performed service, whether at that moment to stand or sit or what. Sandra herself was slow to stand, not clumsy but slowed by her pregnancy. Harry, taking a cue from somebody, was quick to stand. For the first time, Sandra saw that he had a companion. There was a woman with him. She was quick to stand, too, alert and following Harry's lead. That was how

Sandra came to see her; sitting, she had been hidden by Harry's bulk and by the other people. She leaned forward, to pick up the printed order of service, so that Sandra saw her clearly. She was fluffily blonde, a Middle-Western chocolate-box beauty. Sandra knew her face well, although they had never met.

Harry was reunited with the Peach of Nebraska.

The whole congregation was invited, from the pulpit, to a 'meet the new Vicar' party in the Church Rooms immediately after the service. The Church Rooms were opposite the side gate into the churchyard, two doors from the Chestnut Horse, a low white building, incongruously Regency in style, which had been converted between the wars from an orphanage. Presumably there were no longer enough orphans in the area to justify an orphanage. There were not enough attenders at Prayer Meetings, Bible Readings and the like to justify the Church Rooms, either, but they would be full this evening.

Dan Mallett realised with astonishment that he was included in the invitation. That made a kind of first. He thought he would decline it. He had no taste for parochial coffee, and people would assume he was there to nick the spoons.

He could prove to Fiona Muspratt that he had been at the service; he wished he had any other proof than the proof he had.

Fiona Muspratt, with the rest of the choir, processed after the Bishop and clergy into the Vestry at the end of the service. The Vestry was overcrowded, and full of a kind of subdued Anglican jollity. The Bishop was a merry Bishop, who thought it was quite all right to laugh out loud in the Vestry. The choir laughed too, and the Reverend Gordon Hedges, and the sidesmen who were counting the collection.

Fiona laughed with the rest, but her laugh was a false laugh. She could not forget the sudden, abject misery which had blinked on and off in the Vicar's wife's face.

She took off her surplice, and hung it in the cupboard with the rest. She went out into the churchyard, under the yews and the pollarded limes; she had arranged to meet her family in the west porch, and to go with them to the Church Rooms to meet the Vicar.

A small, dark-suited figure materialised among the gravestones, just visible in the light from the open Vestry door. Dan did not walk towards her, or stand up quickly, or jump down from anything: he materialised.

'Bargain ben a bargain,' he said, in the voice that would normally have made Fiona laugh. 'If you'll give me a lift in your car,' he added, in the voice which was like her father's voice, 'the Red Lion in Milchester does the best dinner hereabouts. I don't mean tonight. I'd ask you home, but my mother might eat you.'

'I looked for you in the church,' said Fiona. 'I didn't see you. I don't think you were there. I think you've just been sitting on a grave.'

'Oh, I was there. A rollicking sort of sermon, a bit hearty for an old peasant like me. Unfortunately I can prove I was there.'

'How?'

'Something I saw, which I think you saw, which I don't think anyone else saw. Something I wish I hadn't seen. Something there must have been a reason for, and I think the reason must be horrible.'

Fiona nodded, uselessly in the near-darkness.

'I know exactly what you mean,' she said. 'Yes, horrible. Afterwards she looked sort of dead.'

'An' now she's got to face all the nobs and all the others,' said Dan, 'with a cup of coffee made out of army trousers.'

'Is that what there'll be?'

'Tea might be an option. Brewed out of army boots. You'd need a zinc-lined stomach.'

'You're very delicate, all of a sudden.'

'The gourmet of the grassroots. I've been spoiled, actually.'

'You certainly have. You take an awful lot for granted.'

'I take your honesty for granted. Bargain ben a bargain.'

Fiona did laugh, but it was a small, unhappy laugh.

Dan dematerialised. It was not as though he walked away into the yew trees, but as though they leaned forward and gulped him.

She joined her family in the west porch.

'What a time you've been,' said her mother. 'Who was that you were talking to?'

'I don't know,' said Fiona. 'One of the village. He was asking about the pointing of the psalms.'

She was a little ashamed of lying so glibly, to her own mother, when she was two minutes out of church. But her mother was anxious to be accepted, without delay, into the most resplendent circles in Medwell Fratrorum (from what Fiona had seen, even the most resplendent shone pretty dimly) and having Dan Mallett as a friend of the family sat awkwardly in that programme.

A bargain was a bargain. She would have dinner with Dan. It would be tricky to arrange. She could not imagine how she had been cajoled or hoodwinked into such a weird arrangement. She believed what the Barclays had told her, back in August – that Dan was a pixie, an elf of the trees, not quite of this world, exercising magic and brewing ancient brews not of army boots.

The Church Rooms were crowded. There was a smell of hair-oil and mothballs and something distantly resembling coffee. They stood in line to meet the new Vicar and his wife, as though at an old-fashioned wedding.

It was not too bad, waiting in line, because there were people they knew to talk to. Fiona's mother was quite content to wait, since she could talk at length to the people in front of them and behind them. In front were Sir George and Lady Simpson, elderly people who were by no means in the way of talking to everybody. Sir George had been in the oil business, and they were widely travelled. Behind were Mr and Mrs Calloway – Edwin and Mildred, already, to Fiona's mother – whose garden was altogether too much of a good thing, even though Dan sometimes worked in it. Edwin had never travelled, even when he was in the Army late in the war, but after the war, and before she was married, Mildred had worked for two years in New York. It was the single subject, Fiona thought, about which she was interesting.

They neared the guests of honour, inch by inch. Progress was slow, because people meeting the new Vicar and his wife either wanted to hear the story of their lives, or tell the story of their own. Everybody, it seemed to Fiona, wanted to be something special, to establish at once a special relationship. Elderly ladies clutched Mr Hedges' arm, as though they owned him, or he was saving them from drowning; semi-retired insurance brokers held on to Mrs Hedges' hand, after shaking it, as though they were appearing together in an advertisement. It slowed things up.

Somebody appeared behind Mrs Hedges' shoulder, speaking to her, disdaining the queue. Perhaps he had stood in the queue, and had established a special relationship. Perhaps he alrcady had a relationship – he was an old friend, a relation. He did not look like anybody who would be an old friend of Mrs Hedges; he did not look like any relation she might have had. He was a big man, flashily and fleshily handsome, with a high colour and a quantity of glossy, prematurely grey hair. Fiona thought at first that the hair was too good to be true – it was a wig, or at least a transplant. She decided it was real, though the silver perhaps touched-up; it was like onc of those pampered lawns so perfect that it looked not like grass but like tufted nylon. He wore a jacket of a check which was nearly tartan. There were broken veins on his nose, which was too thick for the rest of his face. That he was a stranger to Fiona was no surprise – they had only been in the village since June. But he was apparently a stranger to everybody else, too. He was an American tourist, somewhat out of season, who had dropped into the ancient church out of curiosity or piety, who had found himself involved in the Service of Induction, who had found himself invited to the Church Rooms.

He was nothing of the kind. He knew Mrs Hedges and she knew him. Even while shaking somebody's hand, she glanced back at him over her shoulder. It happened again. A face that had been open, closed. A face that had been happy, was in despair. A face that had been alive, was dead. This big, arrogant, overweight man was the cause of that blink of anguish in the church.

She was American – they all knew that about her. Fiona was sure he was American. His hair was American – Fiona recognised it from films. His coat was American – she recognised it from advertisements from old *New Yorker*s which were stacked in her boss's reception room. His face was American. It was not exactly foreign, but it was certainly not English. They were both American, and they had known one another. He had popped up out of her past – what past? He had popped up to – to do what?

He withdrew a little way – not far – five feet away. Fiona and her family shuffled forward. Fiona wanted to run away, screaming, but it was important to her mother that they be seen shaking hands with the new Vicar. There was a split-second struggle in Mrs Hedges' face. Fiona, forewarned, saw it. She thought Mrs Hedges had terrific guts. She wanted to help, but she could see no way to help. She wanted Dan Mallett's help in helping, but she could see no way that even Dan could help.

'Be a cryin' shame,' murmured Harry Curtis behind Sandra's shoulder, 'to tell all these good folks you was a bigamist. Saw about you an' the Reverend, in that magazine. Dentist's waitin' room, in Kansas City. Had me a fillin', for eighty-five bucks. You kin pay for that. You kin pay for my ticket home, an' you kin pay my pension. Or what? You know or what. Don't envy your kid, if it's or what. I'll be around. I'm stoppin' in a room over that saloon two doors down. Right neighbourly. You won't go away an' I won't go away. Good to see you, honey.'

To Fiona it seemed she was shaking hands with a dead woman. To other people she seemed quiet, self-contained, perhaps shy. Well, she was in a new place, among strangers, in a strange country. Nebraska was somewhere near the Rocky Mountains, wasn't it? A long way away. It was better to be a little bit shy than too much the other way.

Mrs Hedges made a good impression on the village, who did not think she would tell them how to bring up their children. She made a good impression on the gentry (they thought of themselves, to the last insurance broker in his glamorised cottage, as the gentry) because her manner was cool but respectful. She made a terrible impression on Fiona, who thought she was someone who had been killed.

There was widespread excitement when, the following morning, an American visitor was found dead in the bedroom he had taken over the Chestnut Horse.

3

The body was found by Debbie Chandler, chambermaid at the Chestnut Horse, at eight o'clock in the morning.

Debbie was not usually a chambermaid, at least in October, because there was not usually anybody staying in the bedrooms over the pub. What Debbie did in the ordinary way was to help with the soups and 'Ploughman's Lunches' in the kitchen behind the bar. Ted Goldingham the landlord got her in extra when they had resident guests – she made up the beds, did the rooms and brought them tea if they wanted it. Mr Curtis the American gentleman had not wanted tea, but he had wanted a call. Probably it was worse for Debbie, finding a body with a dagger in the back and blood all over the place, because she wasn't a regular chambermaid. She screamed and screamed, and people came running, and because it happened at the Chestnut Horse the whole village knew everything about everything by the middle of the morning.

Ted Goldingham first of all tried to shut Debbie up, then went and had a look at the bedroom. He sent the boy immediately for the police, and himself stood guard over the room. Jim Gundry the policeman came pounding along within minutes, doing up his buttons, his boots striking sparks off the road. He rang the Station in Milchester, and himself stood guard until the Chief Detective Superintendent came, with a Detective Sergeant and two uniformed officers. They were followed by the fingerprint men, the photographers, the pathologist, the forensic scientist, and at last a closed van with metal shelves in the back.

One set of facts emerged at once; another set took longer, because they had to come from America.

There was a separate staircase to the four bedrooms over the pub, rising from a little back hall that wasn't used for anything.

There was an outside door to this hall, opening on to an alleyway between the pub and a squat cottage called Turners. The landing which served the four bedrooms and the one bathroom could also be reached by another staircase, from the main part of the pub. Ted Goldingham and his wife, between them, could swear that nobody had used those front stairs between opening time and midnight. The time of death was difficult to establish, because Mr Curtis's bedroom was very hot, and had kept the body warm, but it was certainly before midnight. The murderer had therefore used the back stairs. The outside door to the back hall had a Yale lock, which was locked when the body was discovered. Either, therefore, the deceased had left the door unlocked, presumably because he was expecting a visitor, or he had admitted a visitor, whom presumably he knew and who was presumably the murderer, or the murderer had a key.

Keys? There were four, as far as Ted Goldingham knew. One was hanging on the board behind the bar, one was on his own key-ring, and he had given one each to Mr Curtis and the other visitor.

The other visitor was Mrs Cora Smith, a widow, a relative of Mr Curtis, who had been travelling with him in order to get over the recent death of her husband. Her bedroom was next door to the murder room. There was a communicating door, bolted on her side. Mrs Smith had accompanied Mr Curtis to the service in the church, although she was herself a Baptist, and then to the party in the Church Rooms. At the end of the party Mr Curtis had gone straight to the inn, saying that he intended to go straight to bed. Mrs Smith did not return to the inn, not until the following morning. Instead she followed the Reverend, the new one, the one who had just been inaugurated, or whatever the word was. He was alone, because his wife had already left the party. Somebody told Mrs Smith that the Reverend's wife was tired on account of she was pregnant. The Reverend walked alone to a house which Mrs Smith later learned to be that of an Admiral. She did not meet the Admiral, but she did meet the Reverend. She wanted the advice of somebody she could trust, and there was nobody she could trust that she knew nearer than four thousand miles. She talked with the Reverend outside and then inside the Admiral's house. Apparently she fainted, from fatigue and worry and heartache. She did not remember passing out, but she remembered coming to, and being given a hot drink by an elderly lady whom she now knew to be the Admiral's wife.

She had not had anything to drink. She had been brought up in a strict Baptist household; they were all teetotallers, and she remained one. She did not think she had ever passed out like that before: but she had never before found herself in such a horrible position. It was entirely a personal matter, and she did not wish to discuss it with British policemen.

A man came from the American Consulate, and said to the police that Mrs Smith's private misery could have no bearing on the murder, since Mrs Smith had been in the company of the Reverend Hedges, and then unconscious, and then put to bed in an extra spare bedroom in Admiral Jenkyn's house, by Mrs Jenkyn. The police accepted this point, without prejudice to their right and duty to question Mrs Smith further, if information now awaited from America seemed to make this necessary.

The Reverend Gordon Hedges confirmed that he had been approached, as he was walking back from the Church Rooms to the Jenkyns' house, by a fair-haired young woman, then entirely unknown to him, known to him now as Mrs Cora Smith, evidently American, hailing, by remarkable coincidence, from the same state as Mr Hedges' own wife. She was in a state of extreme agitation, approaching collapse. She had, in the whole of Britain, the whole of Europe, nobody who was closer to her than the barest acquaintanceship, except the late Harry Curtis. She was in urgent need of advice and comfort. What she had told him was in the strictest confidence. Mr Hedges was an Anglican priest, not precisely bound by the Seal of the Confessional, but he was bound to respect Mrs Smith's confidence unless he was convinced of the necessity of breaking it. He did not know at exactly what time Mrs Jenkyn had tucked Mrs Smith up in bed.

Mrs Jenkyn gave not too little information but too much. She had lent the poor little thing one of her own nightdresses, which was far too big for the poor little thing, and a pair of her own bedroom slippers, which she could hardly keep on because they were so much too big, and put her to bed in a room which was generally used, that is to say a few times a year, by the Jenkyns' grandson, who always left it like a pigsty, not that they were not glad to see him. She filled up a hot-water-bottle for her new guest, whom she was by that time thinking of as her patient, from the electric kettle in her own bedroom, and tucked it under her poor little cold toes.

It was then just after twenty minutes past midnight, Mrs Jenkyn remembering the time with accuracy because it was so shockingly late for an old body like herself.

Mrs Smith's latchkey to the side door of the Chestnut Horse had been in her bag and was there still. She could not stand to go back to that room. A policewoman packed up her things for her. She was found accommodation in a cottage on the edge of the village which did bed-and-breakfasts in the summer. She, and the man from the Consulate, accepted that she might be needed for further questioning.

A few people remembered having seen the deceased American talking to Mrs Hedges at the party in the Church Rooms. Nobody else remembered having talked to him, and nobody remembered seeing him talk to anybody else.

Mrs Hedges said she had only the dimmest memory of talking to the American. She was excited, and exhausted, and seemed to be meeting hundreds of strangers for a few seconds each. She thought the American had said something conventional, like apologising for kind of gatecrashing a party which was supposed to be just the people of the village. She imagined she had replied equally conventionally, saying that he was welcome, something like that. She admitted that she was not so much remembering her reply as imagining the kind of thing she must have said. Yes, she had slipped away from the party early – the police could see why.

The murder weapon was of Swiss manufacture, the blade heavy, double-edged, razor-sharp and needle-pointed, spring-loaded and normally carried in the grip. It was a very dangerous weapon which nobody had ever seen before. It had no fingerprints on the handle; it had the deceased's prints on the flat of the blade, which had been kept slightly oiled. It was presumably his knife, but Mrs Smith had never seen it. He might have had it for security, hers and his own, on the first trip either of them had made to the dangers of Europe. He might have had it to open letters, but as he had received no letters there was no knowing about that.

Mrs Smith could give an exact account of her journey with Harry Curtis, because there was not so very much to remember.

The trip was Harry's idea – something he had always wanted to do, something she ought to do, to get over her bereavement. It was certainly kindness on his part, or seemed to be, but she guessed it was also fear of loneliness. He was not a man who would want to eat dinner alone in a strange city, let alone one where he couldn't talk the language. They went Dutch. He had a little money, though not enough to splash around; she had a little, and never was the kind to splash it around. They were not for the Ritz or the best seats in a theatre. They got around by train or bus. They flew Omaha to New York, and New York to London. They stayed four days in a small hotel in West Kensington, name found by Harry from some kind of guidebook, reservations made by him. They got cheap seats for two musicals; they went on a guided bus tour, and a trip on a boat up and down the river. They took a train to Milchester. Harry had maybe read about Milchester in his guidebook. They spent a night there, Harry having called from London to make reservations. They saw the Cathedral. Harry made a call, which he said was confirming reservations in the Chestnut Horse in Medwell Fratrorum.

Why? Mrs Smith said Harry said he had read where you didn't see the real England in cities, you had to get to the grassroots, which meant a country village with a crazy name. Mrs Smith didn't want to be rude about the name, but it wasn't like any name she ever heard of in Nebraska. She did not know how Harry had heard of this particular village, or how he knew the name of the tavern. She was pretty sure he had heard of it before they got to Milchester, because he had called not to make reservations but to confirm them. Maybe some magazine article, something in a Sunday travel supplement, had mentioned it and Harry had been tickled by the name. She had gone along with his ideas because she knew nothing whatever about Britain and Harry had at least read about it.

All of this was checked out and it was, of course, exactly true.

It was strange that the very first place they went to from London was Milchester, and the very first place they went to from Milchester was Medwell, and the very first night they spent there he was murdered and she had a kind of breakdown.

It was obvious – in the bar of the Chestnut Horse, as in the Chief Detective Superintendent's office in Milchester – that it was all an impossible coincidence. (These words were used in the Police Station, and different words of similar meaning in the pub.) Something, somebody, had brought Harry Curtis to Medwell, specifically, in preference to any other place. He was killed because of his arrival – because he was who he was – or because of something he did when he got here. What did he have time to do? Who did he even talk to, except Ted Goldingham and Debbie and apparently, for a moment, Mrs Hedges?

He came from Nebraska. She came from Nebraska. Atlases were opened and Nebraska found, right up against the Rocky Mountains. It was chance that brought Mrs Hedges here, all the way to Medwell from Nebraska, no doubt about that – chance that had brought her together with the Reverend Hedges, chance that had brought him to the living in this parish. But him? Harry Curtis? Coming so direct, all that way? How could that be chance?

What kind of a man was Harry Curtis? State and City Police would tell, if there was anything to tell and if they knew about it, via Interpol. Meanwhile you could only go on what he wore, what was in his grips, what Ted Goldingham said about him, and what Cora Smith said about him.

What he had been seen wearing was a little unfamiliar but not communicative of anything at all. He was dressed like a man you might see on TV, in an American sitcom or crime movie. The things in his bags were the things in a tourist's bags. All that was interesting was the absence of anything interesting – there were no notebooks, address books, books or papers of any kind. He must have had names, addresses, telephone numbers, since he had made reservations at three different places, but if so either he had thrown away the piece of paper or he had a photographic memory. It was strange to have *nothing* written down. He was not covering his tracks – his movements were easily traceable – but he was secret about his intentions. Perhaps not deliberately secret, not secret for any sinister reason. Where was he going next? Straight back to Nebraska, having done what he came to England to do? Mrs Smith thought not.

Ted Goldingham and his wife could add nothing. The rooms had been booked by letter from America, typed on hotel paper and postmarked Omaha; Ted only remembered that because he had torn off the stamp to give a kid that collected them. Bookings confirmed, the day before arrival, by telephone from Milchester. The man himself big, friendly enough, quite easy to understand, had a few questions about the time and form of the Service of Induction, which Ted himself had not been able to attend, it being his busy time.

Debbie had hardly met him alive. She had only properly seen him dead.

It made more sense for the police to question Mrs Smith when they had seen what was to be seen from Nebraska.

It was pretty certain that questioning would distress her; it was not certain that she could tell them anything useful. The impression she gave was that she had known Harry Curtis all her life, but never very well. They were relatives but not particularly friends. The reason she had gone along with his suggestion about going to Europe was not because they were intimate, but because it was exactly the right thing to do at that exact moment – if somebody else had made the suggestion, she would have gone with that other person, instead. That was the way it sounded. There was agreement about this, in the bar of the Chestnut Horse as in the Milchester Police Station.

No amount of further questioning, in the village and in the neighbouring villages, produced anything at all.

Turners, the cottage on the other side of the alleyway that ran beside the Chestnut Horse, had no windows on that side. Old Vince Mellins and his wife were in bed and asleep by ten. Even if they had been awake and up and about they would have seen and heard nothing, because of there being no windows that side, and because they could hardly see or hear at the best of times.

The village street more or less started between the churchyard and the Chestnut Horse. Going one way, there was a hundred yards of what you could properly call street, with streetlights, the post office, the greengrocer's, one other shop which had been for sale for nine months, a filling station, and some very pretty cottages occupied at weekends by insurance brokers. In the other direction, the road became a road, passing a few cottages and the cricket ground and the gate into Admiral Jenkyn's garden. There were no lights on the road. On the night of the murder there had been a half-moon, obscured most of the time by cloud. It was not a completely dark night, even when the clouds covered the moon. The Reverend Hedges, for example, said that he had found the way back to the Jenkyns' without difficulty, not using the flashlight which the Admiral had lent him.

The cottages on the road were real cottages, and the people who lived in them had not attended the Service of Induction. None of them could remember looking out of their windows between ten and midnight, and none of them could remember seeing anybody.

A lot of people had seen a lot of people in the other direction, under the streetlights, going from the church to the Church Rooms, going from the Church Rooms to their homes. Nobody had seen anybody going into the side door of the Chestnut Horse. It would have been difficult to see anybody doing this, even if you were watching for it, because the alleyway was very dark.

Mrs Hedges signed a statement, accurately transcribed, in which she said that she had never seen Harry Curtis before the party in the Church Rooms, and that she had never heard the name. It might not be coincidence that Harry Curtis came straight from Nebraska to Medwell Fratrorum, and Mrs Hedges came by a more roundabout route from Nebraska to Medwell Fratrorum; if there was a link Harry Curtis presumably knew about it but, according to her statement, Sandra Hedges did not.

The local questions went on and on, pending answers from America that might not be answers to anything. All the people who had been in church were asked what they had seen, especially those who had arrived at the same time as Harry Curtis and his companion, and those who had left at the same time, and those who had sat within sight of them.

All the members of the choir were asked if they had seen anything relevant, anything at all. Fiona Muspratt was asked.

Fiona knew that she had really seen what she had come to doubt if she had seen. She knew because Dan Mallett had seen it too – had described to her, in words much like those she had used to herself, the change in Mrs Hedges' expression, and the exact moment in the service when it had happened. Dan told Fiona about it because it proved that he had been to the service. It was a strange sort of proof, but it was proof. Fiona was convinced about Dan, and also about herself and about Mrs Hedges.

It was not the sort of thing the police were asking questions about. They were asking about Harry Curtis and what he did and how he acted and who he was looking at and who he spoke to. No question they asked could be answered by describing the change in the parson's wife's face. Fiona did not feel obliged to advance a gratuitous bit of information which was not asked for; and anyway that awful expression might have been caused by a twinge of indigestion or some discomfort associated with having a baby.

Dan Mallett did not advance any information, either, because nobody asked him. Nobody told the police that he was in church; it was possible that nobody saw him there, so great was his capacity for being present without presence.

'If they'd come straight out and asked you,' said Dan to Fiona, 'what would you have said?'

'I've been asking myself that,' said Fiona. 'I don't know.'

They were facing one another over a round table in the Old Mill Restaurant. It was an extraordinary place for Dan to be. He had been there before, many times, but only to the back door. The Old Mill was run by a Wing-Commander of remorseless *bonhomie*, addressed by his regulars as 'Wingco', who bought pheasants without asking where they came from.

Dan had in the event decided against the Red Lion in Milchester, which reminded him too strongly of his slave-time at the bank. The Red Lion had once been a coaching-house; now it belonged to a chain which had revived the coaching-house atmosphere to the extent of sporting reproductions on the walls and lamps in the shape of wrought-iron candlesticks. There was piped music in all the downstairs rooms, and there were apt to be people there who knew Dan by sight and reputation. It was an easy decision not to go to the Red Lion; it was a more difficult one to go to the Old Mill, because it was expensive, and *terra incognita* from the back door frontwards, and because the Wingco had bought anonymous pheasants from Dan quite often over the previous winters. Dan thought the Wingco might not recognise, in a neat-suited, self-effacing Assistant Bank Manager, the inarticulate yokel – something like a ferret in corduroy trousers – who sold him pheasants.

Fiona was not able to come out to dinner with Dan the first or second evenings he asked her, because her parents were expecting her at home and she was reluctant to tell them downright lies. That was Monday and Tuesday. On Wednesday she was genuinely kept late at the office. She was genuinely invited to join a group of colleagues for dinner (at the Red Lion, inevitably). She could genuinely tell her mother so on the telephone. She did not say that she would be dining with her colleagues, but that they had asked her to join them and she would be late. She thought she was being a little devious but not really deceitful. She really did want to have dinner with Dan, but she could not for the life of her think why.

When the rest of them went off merrily to the Red Lion, she got into her car and went to Dan's cottage. It was a bore that he was not on the telephone, but you could not imagine a telephone there. It was a very small cottage, one room downstairs and one and a half upstairs, with no vertical quite upright and no horizontal quite level. It looked as though it was lived in by a witch, and Fiona saw, without surprise, that it was lived in by a witch. She was prepared for Dan having a mother, but not for the malevolent old face which glared at her from a tiny upstairs window.

While Fiona strolled in the woods of which the cottage seemed a freakish outgrowth, Dan transformed himself, astonishingly quickly, from a creature who belonged in such a cottage to a creature who belonged in the Old Mill. She drove him there, refusing to allow him to pay for the petrol. He made her laugh so much, switching from yokel to bank manager and back again, that she nearly went into a tree.

When they stopped in the Old Mill's car-park, Dan thanked her politely for the lift (bank manager), and then nipped out of the car and round to her door, and opened the door for her. She did not remember that anyone had ever done this before. He asked her, slow and shy, to come down out of the carriage (yokel) so that she burst out laughing yet again.

She thought she understood why she had wanted to have dinner with Dan, on top of the fact that she had promised to if he came to church. Nobody she had ever met had made her laugh so much, although she was a girl who laughed often: and nobody she had ever met had such perfect old-fashioned manners.

The Old Mill was indeed an old mill, built beside and over the river six miles from Medwell in the direction away from Milchester. It had been turned into a restaurant by its present owner, who greeted them boomingly in a chintzy hallway. The owner had joke moustaches and little red eyes. It seemed to Fiona that he reacted to Dan with a moment of astonishment.

She asked Dan about this, when they were sitting with drinks waiting to be called to their table.

'Struck by a likeness,' said Dan. 'Fleeting resemblance to a local peasant.'

'Ah,' said Fiona. 'What have you been selling him?'

'According to the Greek philosophers,' said Dan, 'a pirate acquires rights of ownership in his booty, owing to the efforts he

44

puts in to get it. On a strict reading of Greek philosophy, I've sold the Wingco some of my own property.'

'But you're not a pirate.'

'Try telling that to Jim Gundry. He's the one with big boots and a blue uniform.'

They were brought menus. They were both shocked by the prices, but only Fiona said so. Dan had to steer her away from the very cheapest things on the menu, which she tried to choose simply in order to save him money. It was another thing to like very much about her, which made about seven hundred things to like very much about her.

He himself could not afford the five courses he really wanted. Even so the quantity he ate astonished Fiona. She had a healthy appetite, but she ate about a third of what he ate.

'Either you've been starving yourself, or else you're completely hollow,' she said as she saw his cheesecake disappear.

'Neither, really,' said Dan. 'Metabolic mystery. It's worry, actually.'

'What are you worried about?'

It was Mrs Hedges he was worried about, and for the first time that evening they began to discuss it, low-voiced, their dinner finished and their elbows on the table, leaning intimately towards one another so that they could have brushed foreheads.

Over their second cups of coffee, with which came the bill, she told him that she had not lied to the police, any more than she had precisely lied to her mother; she had simply not told either the whole truth.

Dan paid the bill. It was probably the first time for years that cash had been used to pay a bill for dinner in that place. The management were agreeable to accepting cash.

Fiona wondered where the money had come from. She was shocked at how little she was shocked by some of the answers that occurred to her.

Dan, for his part, was not shocked at all by Fiona keeping silent to the police. He was not one for telling anybody everything; in fact, in the ordinary way, he was not one for telling anybody anything. He would have told Fiona almost anything about himself, his life, his mother, his birds and animals, because only a little of all that was secret, and because Fiona was

45

entirely special. But even to Fiona, and even though they were discussing it, he did not tell the important thing he knew about the murder.

He knew that Sandra Hedges had done it.

4

In spite of the delicious proximity of delicious Fiona, Dan's mind flew back, as it had done so very many times, to the evening of the Service of Induction at the Church of All Saints, Medwell Fratrorum.

When the sidesman opened the west door at the end of the service, when most of the congregation were still on their knees, Dan slipped out like a mouse. He was near the door. He was camouflaged in his dark banker's suit. His exit could not have been physically unseen, but it was certainly not noticeable. Other people made a party of leaving the church, in the porch and in the churchyard just outside the porch, to a point which caused a queue to develop of people trying to get out; they asked after one another's arthritis and grandchildren, and the questions took plenty of time to ask and to answer. Dan missed all that. He was out among the ancient graves, many without headstones, simply six-foot cylinders of turf very slightly raised over the level of the turf of the churchyard; the oldest headstones stood at drunken angles, lichen-covered, illegible even at noon. Over them gloomed the yew trees, looking as old as the graves, planted in the Middle Ages to stop the parson grazing his sheep in the churchyard; this was an issue on which parson and patron had differed, and the planting of poisonous trees was the only way for the squire to stop the priest from desecrating the resting-places of the dead.

Dan found himself neutral in this dispute. He did not object to the idea of a sheep grazing on his grave, but he knew his mother would regard it as a liberty.

There was a path between the west door of the church and the door of the Vestry. It was shrouded by yews and crowded by graves. He waited among his ancestors for Fiona. She would be a minute or two. There was a big choir this evening, for this special occasion, and they would all be trying to take off their surplices and hang them up at the same moment, and the choirboys would be jabbering and giggling, and there were Bishops and such. It was no hardship to wait. Dan wanted to see Fiona, even in the dark, and it was not so very dark. It was a dry evening, warm for the time of year; a half-moon blinked between half-speed clouds. Dan was conscious of a feeling of goodwill from the folk underground all about him; this made a nice change – the folk above ground all about him were apt to feel a bilious ill-will.

Whenever he moved, and even when he was still, his face encountered gossamer. The churchyard spiders had laid their eggs in the summer, and their babies had been hatched by the warmth of the sun at midday. Thousands of the tiny creatures were now floating about at the ends of lengths of microscopic silk. Dan knew that when he got home, and under a light, he would find a lot of infant spiders on short pieces of cobweb all over his best banker's suit. He hoped they might be money-spiders, for the sake of the operation on his mother's arthritic hip.

Fiona came towards him, a wayward moonbeam theatrically brushing her hair with silver. For recognising her he did not need the moon. She moved unlike any other member of the choir, not quite like any other member of the human race. She flowed along. She was a gazelle, or a thoroughbred. Wearing heels, she was just about as tall as he was. He was glad she was no taller. He intercepted her, and they talked softly. What they said was not for the rest of the choir, although it did not matter that the dead heard them.

Dan convinced Fiona that he had attended the service. She did not laugh as he had heard her laugh, because they were both thinking about the change in the expression on the face of the new Vicar's wife.

She left him to join her family in the west porch (they were asking after somebody's arthritis and grandchildren) and Dan wondered for a moment whether to accept his invitation to the party in the Church Rooms. He only wondered for a moment. He had not really been invited. It was as though the Archdeacon (Dan thought he was an Archdeacon – he sounded as Dan imagined Archdeacons sounded) had said: 'Everybody in the congregation is invited, except of course Dan Mallett, who is not a proper member of the congregation or of anything else.'

It was true that Dan was not a member of anything, except the Fiona Muspratt Fan Club.

Time was getting on. The Chestnut Horse would be closing soon. Dan found that his bashful contribution to the hymns had given him a thirst. He crossed the churchyard, issuing mental apologies to the graves he stepped over, and went out into the street by the lych-gate. There was a light over the door of the Church Rooms, and lights behind the curtains of the windows. There was a light over the gibbet-hung sign of the Chestnut Horse, and lights in all its downstairs windows. There were lights upstairs, too. Two of the upstairs windows, curtained, had lights behind them.

Dan paused, mildly curious. He intimately knew the geography of the Chestnut Horse, upstairs as well as downstairs, although Ted Goldingham did not know that he knew about the upstairs. The lit windows were bedrooms. It was peculiar that in October there should be guests in the bedrooms. Ted Goldingham did not actually discourage people from staying in his bedrooms, but he did nothing to encourage them, either. They disturbed his routine, and obliged him to pay overtime to Debbie Chandler. He made a bit of profit, but not enough to justify the hassle. He had said so often, behind the bar in his shirt-sleeves. Ted Goldingham was a bore on many subjects, and this was one of them. But here he was with two bedrooms apparently occupied, well after the end of the normal tourist season.

Business gents? The Chestnut Horse had never attracted commercial travellers – they stayed in Milchester, at the Red Lion if it was a big firm, at a bed and breakfast if it was a little one. Somebody who'd bought a house locally, putting up at the pub until their furniture was in? But nobody had bought any houses locally since August. Dan kept abreast with the local real-estate – he could always do with more ruralised Londoners who paid him several pounds an hour for his Thomas Hardy accent and his quirky, homespun proverbs.

Dan brushed a baby cobweb off his eyebrow, and realised that he could find out who was staying in the pub, if he really wanted to know, by going into the pub and asking.

One of the upstairs lights went out. Early to bed, or down to the bar for a nightcap.

Dan hung on his heel, undecided. At least, he thought it was his heel he was hanging on. He was familiar with the phrase, but he did not think he had ever committed the action, or inaction. He was undecided between going into the Chestnut Horse for a pint of bitter, or going home for a glass of whisky. The third possibility, of going into the Chestnut Horse for a glass of whisky, was not a serious proposition because it was an absurdly expensive way to buy whisky. It was too early to go to bed. He was not dressed for doing anything profitable, of any of the sorts of things, which, by night, he found profitable.

There was no light from Turners, the cottage not much bigger than his own where Vince Mellins and his wife lived out their cross old lives. Their garden was a disgrace. Some of the neighbours might have helped, but Vince was too proud to let them. It was a silly sort of pride. Dan's own mother had a lot of points of pride – so many that she was like the young hedgehog Dan had found that morning in a hole intended for a water-butt: a hedgehog which rolled itself into a ball of spikes, as Dan's mother mentally did, and watched his every movement with bright suspicion, as she also did – but she once had a Police Sergeant from Milchester digging the potato-patch in her garden. The Sergeant was waiting for Dan, who was sitting in some bracken waiting for him to go away. All three of them knew that that was how it was, and Dan's mother was the only one who turned the situation to advantage. Dan wasted that whole afternoon, although he enjoyed the sight of the Sergeant perspiring with the spade.

Now Dan was wasting a whole evening. He did not mind wasting an occasional evening. Most people wasted every evening and night of their lives.

Everybody that was going to the Church Rooms had now gone there, and some people were already coming out again. It was evidently not a party people wanted to linger at. A second cup of coffee was unlikely and a third unthinkable.

Dan recognised most of the people who came out; they were lit by the open door of the Church Rooms. It was impossible to recognise everybody, because they came out in clumps.

Something mildly peculiar happened. In a small way it disrupted the pattern. Everything – the people having arrived, the people leaving – was happening predictably, but something was happening contrariwise. It was probable that nobody noticed, and Dan was sure that nobody was meant to notice. There was a member of one of the chattering clumps outside the Church Rooms, who went not away to his cottage or his car but into the Church Rooms, and who had arrived not from the Church Rooms but from elsewhere. All right, he was late for the party. Coming from where? Coming from the alleyway that led in pitch darkness between the Chestnut Horse and the Mellins's cottage.

That was a rum place to come from. The alley led to the back yard of the pub; from there you could get to the back door of the pub, the outbuilding now a garage where Ted Goldingham kept his car, and the other outbuilding that was now the Gents'. In the alley itself you found the side door of the pub, from which you reached the bedrooms. The man who had unobtrusively emerged from the alley joined a group in the light. He was clearly visible and instantly recognisable. He was sixtyish, handsome in a way that made overstatement of understatement; it was Terence Barclay, for whom Dan did occasional genteel gardening, by whose pool he had first seen Fiona Muspratt.

What in God's name was Terence Barclay doing in the back of the Chestnut Horse? He was trying to steal Ted Goldingham's car? He had cars of his own, better than Ted's. He was going to the Gents'? Obviously possible, after coffee in the Church Rooms, but why go so far? The Church Rooms had a Gents' of its own more salubrious than the pub's. Terence Barclay didn't know that, being a relative newcomer, probably never having been to the Church Rooms before? Or was there a queue of near-nobs waiting to unload the Church Rooms coffee? Possible; not very likely; most of these people were minutes from their homes.

He'd been to see one of the people in the bedrooms of the Chestnut Horse.

Somebody was there, sure enough: two lights had been on and one was on still.

There was nothing weird about it, and probably nothing fishy about it. Terence Barclay knew – had known for weeks – that a friend was staying in a room over the pub. Why not ask the person to his house? Unpresentable person – tart, low-grade salesman, seedy racecourse acquaintance. Discreet place to meet. You leave a milling crowd, you rejoin the milling crowd, nobody notices you've been away. If you're challenged for an alibi (by your wife, for instance) you just say, 'I was at the party all the time – I spoke to X, Y and Z. They'll tell you.'

He was furtive about it. To Dan, watching closely for no good reason, he was obtrusively unobtrusive. His reason for going wherever he had gone was secret if not guilty.

In Dan's experience, handsome middle-aged men were secretive about girls, boys or money. Terence Barclay was not worried about money (Dan had that on Lady Simpson's authority) and Dan was sure he was not a bloke for boys. It was likely, then, that he had a girl in one of those bedrooms over the pub. Good luck to him. Dan was not curious about other people's girls, unless he wanted them himself. He did not think he wanted any girl who stayed at the Chestnut Horse.

The girl he wanted was not to be seen.

Dan saw the Vicar's wife, coming out with Admiral and Mrs Jenkyn. The Vicar was not with them. She had an excuse to slip away early, but he had to stay to the end. No doubt he was hoping the end was near. It was near. The superior parson Dan had labelled an Archdeacon came out, and went off to wherever he had parked his car. Some time afterwards the new Vicar came out. He strode away briskly in the other direction, towards the Jenkyns' house where they were stopping. He would be there in a few minutes. He strode away like a man who enjoyed striding. Probably he enjoyed gardening, and carpentry and pointing brickwork. Whether he enjoyed these things or not, he would probably do them for himself, because parsons were paid so little. The new Vicarage garden would not feel the penetration of Dan's leisurely fork, nor its cupboards his dawdling hammer. He would not be allowed in the Vicarage or its garden, unless he had come to unburden his soul.

Nobody was allowed in Vince Mellins's garden. But somebody was there, in the narrow patch of jungle in front of the cottage. A burglar? Nobody would want to burgle that cottage. A tramp? Tramps didn't lurk in cottage gardens. A teenage vandal? Unlikely; and the garden could do with a bit of destruction.

There was not enough light to see what was moving: only that there was movement.

Dan was standing by the churchyard wall, under a yew that grew just the other side of the wall. His suit was dark against dark brick and dark tree-trunk. There was a streetlight twenty feet away, but the yew shadowed his face. He was not deliberately invisible, but he had the habit of invisibility, and the habit held even when, for once, he was doing nothing illegal.

It was a person, yes. It was not a cat or a cow. The person was making an attempt at stealth, which if anybody but Dan had been watching would have been a pretty good attempt: but Dan's night vision was exceptional because, he supposed, he used his eyes at night more than most people. The person went round the end of the sagging fence and into the alleyway by the Chestnut Horse. She was there swallowed up by darkness that even Dan's eyes could not penetrate. Dan would hardly have seen the movement if he had not been staring and waiting; he would hardly have heard the stealthy footsteps on the flagstones of the alley.

She, yes, no question of that. Coat over a skirt, shawl or scarf over her head. Female movement. Young female movement, somehow. Not so very graceful, not like the lovely liquid movements of Fiona Muspratt. A kind of young clumsiness. Not the clumsiness of a child, but that of a . . . Dan was aware of having seen a certain heaviness, a lethargy in the movements of young women who were not normally oafish or idle. It was when they were having babies, when they were getting large. What girls were having babies in the village? Dan could think of a few, some married. He could imagine no reason that would bring any of them, at ten-thirty on an October night, into Vince Mellins's garden or the alleyway by the pub.

There was a brief glow in the alleyway, its source just out of Dan's sight. The side door of the pub, opened for somebody to go in or somebody to go out. Dan visualised the little hallway, with a single dim bulb in a bracket on the wall. It led to nothing except the back stairs, and they led to nothing except the four bedrooms. It was an absurd bit of design, caused by a man enlarging the building who ran out of money. A pregnant woman, going very stealthy, going up the back stairs to one of the bedrooms over the Chestnut Horse. All right, she was staying there. The light that was on was hers, or the one that had been turned off, or a third.

Inherently (Dan framed the word a little nervously to himself – he had not used it out loud for a very long time) there was nothing amazing about any of this, except the stealth. Well, a girl was visiting, on the sly, a tourist who was putting up at the pub. There were girls in the village – in every village Dan ever heard of – who were happy to earn a few quid from visiting strangers. But not when they were eight months pregnant. The man was the father of the child. Stealth because she had a husband who thought he was the father. If it was that sort of tangle, Dan didn't want to hear about it.

It was rum, all this traffic in and out of the side door of the Chestnut Horse – rum at any time of day, at any time of the year, most peculiar late on an October evening. Terence Barclay had come and gone. Was the pregnant girl going to the same place? Seeing the same person? Was she looking for him? Had he been looking for her? Was he the father of the baby?

Dan thought it was still something he didn't want to hear about, but he stood waiting and watching.

Closing time at the Chestnut Horse. A yellow oblong appeared in the wall under the sign, occupied by successive silhouetted figures coming out into the village street. Dan recognised some of the silhouettes. The oblong disappeared; Ted Goldingham was locking up.

The lights were going off in the Church Rooms, too. The party had trickled away some time before, and old Hilda Voakes had been clearing up after it. Dan had missed it all, pub and party both, hanging about among gravestones with cobwebs on his face.

He realised that he had been hoping for another glimpse of Fiona Muspratt. It was the kind of thing you did when you were fourteen. Dan derided himself for dangling after a superior girl who was miles out of his reach. At least it explained why he seemed to be caught outside the churchyard, like the hedgehog that had fallen into the hole outside his cottage.

No other light came on from the pub, from the bedroom windows over the alley. That suggested that the pregnant girl had gone to the room that was already lit. Or she had gone out leaving the light on, and had now returned to her bedroom. Ted Goldingham wouldn't like that. He talked about fuel conservation, but what he meant was his bills. If it was her room, why was she so anxious not to be seen?

Why had Terence Barclay been so anxious not to be seen, coming out of the alley and rejoining the party?

It was obvious by now that the Muspratts, like some others, had gone out by the side door of the Church Rooms, presumably because their car was in that direction. He had been held by lust, or infatuation, or whatever you called what he felt for Fiona; now he was held by curiosity. The evening was full of oddities.

The periphery of Dan's consciousness was nudged by something. Somebody else was hanging about too, but not in Vince Mellins's garden and not, Dan thought, in the churchyard. He did not know where. He did not, as far as he knew, see the other person, or hear him. He sensed him. This was impossible, since sight and hearing were the relevant senses. The corner of his eyes had caught a glimpse, or the corner of his ear a whisper. He looked and listened. He was good at looking and listening, but he saw and heard nothing.

The evening was fuller of oddities than ever.

It could be assumed, without confidence, that the watcher was watching for what Dan found he was now watching for (having missed Fiona Muspratt) – the reappearance of the pregnant lady who was visiting somebody, perhaps, in a bedroom over the Chestnut Horse. Dan had been about to stifle his curiosity and stop watching, since the circumstances were probably seedy and almost certainly unprofitable. But the presence of another watcher, if there really was one, changed his mind. Even if there were no other watcher – only a cat or a cow – he found that his mind had changed. Invisible under the yew tree, he looked and listened.

He thought he would have been better employed doing anything else he could think of, but he stayed and looked and listened.

It was very quiet. A wind at a high altitude was still pushing the clouds across the face of the sinking moon, but there was no wind in Medwell. There was no sound. The other watcher, if there was one, was as motionless as Dan.

There was a click from the alleyway. No light, but a click, the noise of a door being pulled shut against the spring of a Yale lock. Dan was not sure if he heard footsteps or imagined the sound of the footsteps there must be. The stealthy figure reappeared, barely visible, coat over skirt and something over her head. She looked left and right, almost comically furtive, like somebody in a silent film. Her movements were young but somehow laborious. She had been inside the Chestnut Horse for twenty minutes, according to Dan's internal timer.

His eyes now thoroughly used to the darkness, he recognised her. She was indeed heavily pregnant. He was completely astonished. It was the new Vicar's wife. There was no doubt about it. Dan could not see which of her expressions she was wearing, the one that was full of life or the one that was full of death. She walked away softly, in the incomplete darkness, towards the Jenkyns' house.

The play had ended, and Dan wished he had not seen any of it. If something came out about it, he would hear. If nothing came out, nobody would hear from him. He had liked the look of the Vicar's wife, and for her sudden misery he had felt an unusual stab of compassion. If what was wrong for her had been put right, Dan was pleased and he would not jeopardise the rightness; if what was wrong was still wrong he would not make it worse.

He went off to get his bicycle, trying unsuccessfully to put the whole thing out of his mind.

He bicycled slowly, the chain ticking on its sprocket and the

56

tyres whispering on the road. Above him he was aware of a multitude of beating wings. Fieldfares or redwings, perhaps, come down for the winter from their breeding grounds far inside the Arctic Circle. In the old days it was sport to lime them. Little birds arrived exhausted, after their gigantic flight across the Arctic Ocean, and settled on twigs in the dark or the dawn, and then found that they were stuck. Even Dan's father, even his grandfather, violently disapproved of birdlime. Certainly they knew how to make it and use it – Dan himself knew how to make it – a scentless and nearly invisible glue which caught and held the little birds' feet. They struggled, baffled and terrified. Their struggles made their state worse, because their plumage got stuck in the lime, their breasts and tails and wings. When the sun rose they could be picked off the branches as easily as apples, and put in cages or eaten or turned into playthings for innocent, heartless children.

People could be caught like that. The Vicar's wife's face, there in church, said that she had been caught like that. She settled on her twig in Medwell Fratrorum, the safest place in the world, after voyaging half around the world, and instead of the smooth safe bark of a twig she found her feet in insidious glue. Had she panicked, like the little birds, and made her situation more desperate? Or prised herself away from the birdlime with some enormous, convulsive effort?

Perhaps her stealthy visit to the Chestnut Horse had nothing to do with the expression Dan had seen on her face. Objectively this was possible, but only barely . . .

Putting the whole thing out of his mind was something he failed to do, while he was bicycling, and letting out his dogs for their last run, and drinking a nightcap (malt whisky half-in-half with water from the well) while trying not to wake his mother.

He heard the news at ten-thirty the following morning, while he was pretending to work in Sir George Simpson's garden. Lady Simpson came back from the post office, driving a Range Rover which the Simpsons' lives made more than usually ridiculous. She almost scampered across the lawn to tell Dan. She told him all she knew, which was exactly as much as the whole village knew, which was as much as Ivy Goldingham knew, Ivy having popped round to the post office the minute it opened.

Dan could stop pretending to work for a bit, and did so.

A lot of questions were answered, although the answers were horrible. A new question bothered him, one of the highest importance: who was that other watcher by the graves, supposing that there had really been one, and how much did he know, and how, if at all, was he connected with the Vicar's wife, and what was he going to do about it? Not one question, he realised, but a mounting list of questions, as in the examinations he had sat at the Grammar School; and the last was the most important.

Dan knew exactly what he himself was going to do, which was nothing. He would keep his eyes and ears open, as he always did and a bit extra; that was all. The bluebottles would have to manage without him.

He contemplated the spade in his hand, and thought of graves and grave-diggers.

Harry Curtis, said Lady Simpson, had come to Medwell all the way from a place called Nebraska. Funnily enough, that nice little Mrs Hedges came from Nebraska. Sir George and Lady Simpson had met the new Vicar and his wife the previous evening, and – fancy! – they must have brushed shoulders, literally *brushed shoulders*, with a man who within an hour was horribly murdered!

'Ben a girt road 'at bloke 'a cam,' said Dan, in the voice that represented his grossest overacting, 'fur t'be stucken wi' a girt daggie. 'Tes shame, seemingly, 'at bloke didn' bide home.'

'We all wonder who can possibly have done such a thing,' said Lady Simpson.

Dan agreed that it would be right nice to know.

Lady Simpson was one of those who got out an atlas to find out where Nebraska was. She brought the atlas out on to the lawn to show Dan, which she was able to do after successfully distinguishing Nebraska from Nevada. Dan kept his muddy fingers off the nice clean atlas. The rest of the morning passed in speculation and cups of coffee.

By noon the following day much had been added to public

knowledge of the crime, though not nearly enough. On the day after that Dan saw for the first time the murdered man's companion, said to be his relative, Mrs Cora Smith, who was now putting up with Amy Crate at The Brambles. Amy said she was sweetly pretty, and Dan cautiously endorsed this view. She was too fluffy and kittenish for his taste – more like a Cora than like a Smith; she looked as though she would make whimsical remarks about the expressions on the faces of cars, their smiles or snarls – but in a blonde, soap-flakes-advertising sort of way you had to grant she was pretty. She was young to be a widow, younger than Dan himself, hardly thirty. She had come to England with the deceased in order to get over her bereavement. Everybody knew this, because she told several people about it, after she had told the Reverend Hedges and Admiral and Mrs Jenkyn and the police. She did not want anybody to think she was hard-hearted, gallivanting around in Europe with the husband hardly cold in his grave. It was because she cared too much that she was here, not because she cared too little. This was generally believed, and Dan saw no reason to disbelieve it.

The late Harry Curtis's idea had been to spend at least two weeks in Britain, Cora Smith thought, before crossing over to France. Now that she was here she would stay. She liked the village and its people, and never in her life had she been shown so much kindness. There was so much cruelty in the world that kindness was something you noticed. The village patted itself on the back, and the men in the Chestnut Horse and the women in the post office told one another how kind they all were. Meanwhile Cora Smith was regarded as an asset to Medwell, with her fair prettiness and her dainty clothes.

She was afraid people would think she was hard-hearted, staying in a town (she said Medwell was a town, which nobody had thought of before) where her relative had been brutally murdered by a passing hobo, or a madman, or somebody on the run from prison. But she had been made to feel she was among friends, and it was a moment when she needed friendship. The village agreed that it was her friend, and she was asked to tea by the wives of a number of insurance brokers.

Mrs Jenkyn and the Reverend Mr Hedges were her first

friends in those parts, and remained her best friends. Neither she nor the Reverend Hedges revealed anything about their conversation on the night of the murder, when she had been so upset that she actually fainted. It was supposed that it might have been something dreadful about Harry Curtis, in which case of course she would not wish to speak ill of the dead; or it might be something about her late husband, in which case her feelings were to be regarded as sacrosanct.

She seemed shy when you first met her – she was not at all one of those pushy, brazen women in American television serials – but she thawed when she encountered kindness. Without being exactly secretive, she said very little else about herself. She explained this by saying she was just a small-town homebody, and she was more interested in talking about almost anything else. She let fall a few things, which were poured into the cistern of public knowledge: her husband had been a little older than herself; she preferred dogs to cats and chocolate ice-cream to vanilla; she had acted in an amateur production of *Philadelphia Story*, which was a brave thing to have done on account of her strict Baptist upbringing; in music she preferred the oldies, and the hymns of her childhood could still reduce her to nostalgic tears; she liked home cooking, such as corn fritters and deep-dish apple pie; she had never eaten an oyster, played cards, or smoked a cigarette. Both Dan and Fiona Muspratt heard all this, Fiona some of it from Cora Smith herself. Neither saw anything to dislike about her; neither thought she was very interesting, in spite of coming from so far away, although Fiona was reluctant to say aloud anything so uncharitable.

Terence Barclay's visit to the bedrooms of the Chestnut Horse was explained, though Dan did not explain it to Fiona.

It was nothing whatever to do with the murder, and it was nothing to do with Sandra Hedges. Terence Barclay was a randy old man with a roving eye, a boring wife, and a lot of money. He met a bit of available fluff at the party in the Church Rooms, who had the merits of being young and pretty and willing, and the extra merit of being a bird of passage.

Cora Smith turned out to be not a bird of passage but a winter visitor, like the fieldfares and redwings. She was caught on a limed twig, too, though hers was probably more comfortable than Sandra Hedges' twig. Terence Barclay would make Cora comfortable, and go on doing it whether he liked it or not. He probably liked it fine. They might be meeting at Court Farm or Amy Crate's or somewhere in Milchester or (most likely) a motel some distance away.

As far as Dan knew, nobody knew anything about it except himself. He felt neither censorious nor disapproving. He was sorry for anybody who was driven to buying what should only be given freely, and sorry for anybody driven to selling something that should be happily given.

'I don't know,' said Fiona, over the empty coffee-cups. 'I think I'd tell myself I might have imagined that look on her face.'

Dan nodded. It was probably exactly the right line to take. It didn't matter what he himself said or didn't say, because no policeman would ever believe anything he said; but Fiona would be believed.

Presumably Mrs Jenkyn would give Mrs Hedges an alibi, if it came to that, thinking she was telling the truth; but it would not be a very good alibi, and the police would realise that immediately. It was much, much better that the question should never arise. Fiona did not know as much as Dan did, but she knew enough for questions to arise.

Fiona took Dan in her car to the mouth of the track which led to his cottage. He tried to kiss her in the darkness of the car when she stopped. It was thoroughly awkward, she being behind the steering wheel. She was not surprised, shocked or revolted by his attempt, but amused by it.

'Glad to be a source of merriment,' said Dan, nettled at the outcome of a scene which he had planned in different terms.

'You are,' she said.

She kissed him on the nose, and said good-night. Dan was dismissed. He decided there was something to be said for fluffiness and kittens. He had never met a girl who was completely immune from him except as a source of amusement. He thought grumpily that it was probably good for him, but he didn't like things that were good for him. The last thing he heard as she drove away was her laughter.

5

It was probably not intended that the report from America should become so very public so very soon. But there were many doors, in Milchester and in Medwell, at which this breech of confidentiality could be laid. The Milchester CID had had occasion for secrecy, when co-operating with Scotland Yard or even when acting on its own. There was the case of the pot being grown in a cottage garden, when catching the grower red-handed (or 'green-handed', as the Milchester *Argus* put it in a piece of jocose court reporting) required the absolute discretion of several people for several days. There were cases of smuggling, illegal immigrants, cattle rustling, and receiving stolen goods. Murder investigations were usually conducted in the glare of local spotlights, because they made better news and better gossip, and interviews were given quite as eagerly as they were demanded – very little except murder brought the national press to Milchester, and policemen were as keen as anybody to have their efforts appreciated. It also helped to win the confidence and co-operation of the public. The feelings of Mrs Cora Smith, if nothing else, would on this occasion have inclined the CID towards secrecy; but when you had telex operators, and bits of paper drifting around the office, and reporters from London filling the saloon bar of the Red Lion, something so very astonishing was bound to be hinted at.

Ivy Goldingham, plying like a ferry between the Chestnut Horse and the post office, said she had guessed it all along. PC Gundry said in that case she should have told him.

Mrs Sandra Hedges, when asked both officially and unofficially, said she supposed there were criminals in Nebraska as well as everywhere else, but as far as she knew she had never met one. She said she did not know how you told a criminal when you saw one, unless he was actually committing a crime at the time. It was unnerving enough, she said, to have been talking to someone – even though it was only a few conventional words – who was stabbed to death less than an hour later; it was even odder to find that you had been talking to a convicted criminal with a long record of petty crime and two short stretches in jail.

There had been a delay, over there in Nebraska, because the State Police had needed the dead man's fingerprints – 'Harry Curtis' seemed to have existed only intermittently, as a name with which to get jobs, open checking accounts, and have a passport issued to. He had used so many other names that there was doubt about which was the original.

As Harry Curtis he had never been convicted of anything. Mrs Cora Smith had known him since she was a kid, and always as Harry Curtis; whatever he did under other names, in other parts of the state, was quite unknown to her. It came as a shock, a horrible surprise. Harry Curtis had eaten dinner, in her home, with her folks. Her parents would turn over in their graves if they knew they had entertained a hoodlum. Probably they would have undergone Baptism, by complete immersion, all over again, to wash away the taint of sin.

Mrs Cora Smith's cornflower-blue eyes opened wide in dismay at her own innocence, her gullibility, at the thought of herself travelling with a man like that. How could she not have seen through him, she with her professional training and all? The answer was that Harry Curtis, as a name and a personality, was front man for all the rest. He had to keep the credibility, which meant that while he was using the name he had to keep straight.

Mrs Cora Smith accepted the logic of this, but still she said she was amazed at her own blindness. Ivy Goldingham was amazed at it, too, as she said in the post office not once but a hundred times.

Dan Mallett was amazed not at Cora's innocence but at the success of her act. People thought fluffy kittens must be silly or blind. They could have sharp eyes. This fluffy kitten was for sale, at least to Terence Barclay. She might have kept Harry Curtis, she might have been kept by him – she might have been his employer or his slave. It was impossible to believe that she knew nothing about his criminal past. Dan agreed with Ivy Goldingham, a thing which had seldom happened before. There must have been so many gaps in Harry Curtis's life – such a discontinuity in that personality, while he was away nobody knew where, doing nobody knew what – that questions must surely have asked themselves. Nobody disappeared and re-appeared without anybody wondering where he had been and why. Dan himself, as unassertive as a mouse, could not disappear for more than a day or two at a time without his absence being noted and enquired into. Perhaps it was different in America – perhaps there you could be swallowed up by a city, and come back after six months saying you had been working in the city. Nobody would believe that of Dan – nobody would believe he had been in a city, and nobody would believe he had been working.

As to recognising a professional criminal, the way Ivy Goldingham said she had, Dan was not sure if he would do it in five minutes, but he backed himself to do it in five days, let alone the twenty-five years that Mrs Cora Smith said she had known, slightly known, the late Harry Curtis. Most of the professional criminals Dan knew were neither very professional nor so very criminal; they were people like old Curly Godden, who received the stolen goods his wife nicked from the Milchester supermarkets; they were people, come to that, like himself, and he wondered what Fiona Muspratt thought she was doing having dinner with a villain like him.

Mrs Cora Smith got more invitations rather than fewer, to the gracious converted cottages in the village street, because she had been the victim of such gross and sustained deception. The ladies were atwitter at the thought of travelling with such a man. They were used to travelling with their husbands, none of whom had been to prison, none of whom owned a knife like Harry Curtis's commando dagger.

As a matter of form, as an obvious precaution, the Nebraska police were asked to check out Mrs Cora Smith and Mrs Sandra Hedges. Nothing was on any file about either. Mrs Hedges, as Miss Sandra Lock, had indeed been Assistant Librarian in her home town's public library, and had travelled to Europe, like so many young people, on a little money left to her by her father. It was all exactly as she said. Mrs Cora Smith was a registered nurse, under her maiden name of Cora Lindstrom. She had been married, and had lived, during the brief period of her marriage, in the neighbouring state of Iowa; there was nothing on any file about her there, either, or about the late Elbert Smith.

Really nothing was known about either of these two attractive females from a far place, except that the meagre ascertainable facts bore out everything they said about themselves. It was all pretty irrelevant, since Mrs Hedges had an alibi from Mrs Jenkyn and the Reverend Gordon Hedges, in that order, and Mrs Smith had an alibi from the same people in the other order.

With special knowledge (possibly irrelevant) Dan worked it out differently. He was sure Cora Smith had not gone straight from the party in the Church Rooms to catch and confess to the Reverend Gordon Hedges. She had gone via her bedroom in the Chestnut Horse, to entertain (for what could hardly have been twenty minutes) her new client. It made no difference to the circumstances of the murder or the identity of the murderer. It probably made a difference to what Cora Smith poured out to the parson; that might have been a sobbing confession about Terence Barclay. Dan thought not: but if it was, the Vicar was quite right to keep quiet about it, and to go on doing so as long as possible.

The regulars in the Chestnut Horse wondered, loudly and often, what had brought Harry Curtis to Medwell. Dan wondered about this, too, and he wondered who had shared the churchyard with him on the night of the murder.

Dan supposed that Mrs Hedges' face had changed from live to dead because she had spotted Harry Curtis in the congregation. He supposed that, now that he was dead, it would remain alive. He could not judge, because they moved in different circles. But Fiona Muspratt moved in the same circles as Mrs Hedges did; she told Dan that Mrs Hedges did not look as terrible as she had at one moment in the service, but she did not look as marvellous as she had earlier in the service. Fiona said that she seemed preoccupied, which people put down to the imminence of her first baby; Fiona's mother said that she

66

herself had felt preoccupied when she was having Fiona. Dan understood that Mrs Hedges would be feeling preoccupied.

Dan saw Fiona as often as he could manage, which was not as often as he would have wished, on account of her having an office job on weekdays and moving in different circles at weekends. When they did have a meeting, always of Dan's contrivance, she goaded him into alternating personalities, into performances of his rustic-clown recitations, and she laughed and laughed. None of these meetings was of a kind which would end with him trying to kiss her, or of her kissing him dismissively on the nose.

It was a terrible shame about Fiona, and it was driving Dan crazy. It was a terrible shame about Mrs Hedges, too, and it was probably driving her crazy. Dan could see no way to improve or even influence either situation. He was not used to feeling helpless, and he hated it.

Dan's mother said he was surly, and she ate even less than usual as a way of showing her displeasure. Dan felt guilty about being surly, and worried about his mother eating so little, but try as he might he could do nothing about those things, either.

The police announced that an early arrest was expected. Nobody in the bar of the Chestnut Horse believed them.

Nobody suspected Mrs Sandra Hedges of violence, because she was pretty and pleasant-spoken and pregnant and the wife of the new parson, and because Mrs Jenkyn had known where she was all evening. Nobody suspected her of anything, but opinion in the Chestnut Horse was hardening that the late Harry Curtis had come to Medwell because of her. She did not know the reason; nobody might ever know the reason; but Nebraska was simply too far away for the coincidence to be acceptable.

Dan Mallett, semi-visible in the corner, listened to them adding two and one and making three. He wondered how soon somebody would find the missing digit, and make it four.

67

Dan remembered that, when he was bicycling home on the night of the murder, there had been a few cars on the road. He wondered if any of the drivers had seen anything, not knowing what they were seeing, not knowing that there was anything to see, not knowing they might have impaled a murderer, or the witness to a murder, on their headlights.

The police, logically enough, had evidently been wondering the same thing. They issued appeal after appeal. Several people came importantly forward. They were all locals, on local journeys. Some were going from the Church Rooms to their homes outside the village. Of those, all had already been interviewed by the police. To the police they could add nothing to what they had said; to their friends they could add more stories.

Then the exception appeared, first telephoning the Milchester police, then being questioned by his local police, then turning up in Milchester, most helpful and concerned, then coming with the police to Medwell to show them exactly what he had seen and where and when.

The new witness was called Mr Edward Turnbull, and he owned an antique shop in Plymouth. He had driven to London on business, coming back with the boot of his car full of bric-à-brac he had bought in the Portobello Road. He would be restoring the stuff during the winter, and putting it on sale in next summer's tourist season. He had come by way of Milchester – not so far off his road – because a friend of his was in a nursing home there recuperating from an operation on a toe. Leaving the friend when the nurses turned him out, he had had a snack in the Red Lion – a drink? Just the one: he was not admitting to more – and had headed back to the Exeter road, by the way that ran beside Medwell. Here, at this spot, give or take fifty yards, between the church and the river: a man, dodging behind a tree to get out of the glare of the headlights, but being slow about it. Ten-thirty, ten-forty-five, give or take a quarter of an hour. It was impossible for Mr Turnbull to say whether the man was proceeding towards the village, the church and the pub, or away, because all the movement Mr Turnbull saw was off the road and over the ditch and behind the tree. He had assumed a tramp, or somebody wanting to urinate after leaving the pub. He had thought no more about it. His wife had showed him a piece in the paper, so here he was, glad to accept some expenses but wanting no other reward than the sense of doing his duty as a citizen.

The only man known to have walked along that road at that hour was the Reverend Gordon Hedges. He was known to have done so in the company of Mrs Cora Smith, who had caught him up just after he left the Church Rooms. His presence, on that road then, required the bending of Mr Turnbull's timing, but Mr Turnbull was content to have his timing bent. It didn't help. Mr Hedges was not alone, and would not have dodged behind a tree.

Mr Turnbull could give only the sketchiest description of the man he had seen, not realising at the time that he was looking at a murderer. In fact he could only say one thing with certainty: the man had thick white hair. It might have been pale blond hair. Presumably the hair had been visible, six or so feet above the ground, in the glare of the headlights reflected off the road. In that sort of light it was impossible to distinguish between white and pale yellow hair.

The Reverend Gordon Hedges' hair was not white or straw but a strong brown.

There was one man with strong, white, naval hair who had gone down that road, after dark, away from the village towards the river. But Admiral Jenkyn had walked with his wife and with Mrs Hedges, and the three of them had left the Church Rooms at least three-quarters of an hour – perhaps an hour and a half – before Mr Turnbull had seen the man he had seen.

Admiral Jenkyn's brief statement was taken out and dusted off.

They had walked from his house to the church because neither he nor his wife could see to drive in the dark, and because it was good for them to walk, and because the Hedges had wanted to walk. Consequently they had walked home again. On reaching home, Admiral Jenkyn felt very tired, overwhelmed with sleep. He said good-night to his wife and to Mrs Hedges, left messages of apology to the new Vicar, and took himself to bed. He had seen nobody until breakfast the following morning. The Jenkyns had had separate rooms for years, because with their sleeping pills they both snored. Sometimes they said their good-nights upstairs, but on this occasion Mrs Jenkyn stayed down, or up, because of the Hedges, and Admiral Jenkyn saw nobody from the moment he started up the stairs.

It would be perfectly possible for an active man to climb out of Admiral Jenkyn's bedroom window, on to the roof of a coal-shed, and so to the ground. It would be possible to climb up again, too. Not for him, said Admiral Jenkyn. Forty-five years ago, when he was a midshipman, but not for many years now.

Had he spoken to the late Harry Curtis, at the party in the Church Rooms? He thought he had exchanged a word with him, so conventional as to be immediately forgotten.

Other people confirmed that Admiral Jenkyn had been seen speaking briefly to the stranger in funny clothes.

Mrs Jenkyn confirmed that her husband snored, that he could not possibly have climbed out of and into the house over the coal-shed roof.

There was no conceivable link between the Admiral and a petty crook from Nebraska.

Wait. Admiral Jenkyn had seen no need to mention the matter to the police, who had not asked about it, but it was known in the village that he had spent a period, some years before his promotion and his retirement, in the office of the Naval Attaché in Washington. Was Washington near Nebraska? Out came the atlases again. Well, no. But people went from Washington, which was unpleasantly hot in the summer, for vacations in the Rocky Mountains. They went to Colorado. There was Colorado, next door to Nebraska.

Yes, the Admiral had been to Colorado, a walking and fishing holiday with some male colleagues in the Embassy, wives left behind. Which colleagues? The Admiral remembered three or four of the five or six names. Could the three or four be contacted? They were all, as it happened, dead. They were older than Admiral Jenkyn; he had been the baby of the party.

The date of the trip to Colorado could only be determined by looking at ancient diaries. The date was confirmed, by looking at ancient letters, by Mrs Jenkyn, who had not wanted to go fishing in the Rockies. At that date, Harry Curtis would only just have been adult, but he would have been old enough to have started his shadowy career.

Another digit was found to add to the two and the one to make a most astonishing four.

Clearly, Admiral Jenkyn had gone to Nebraska or Harry Curtis had gone to Colorado (people presumably did both things all the time) and the Admiral had had it off with a girl in a motel, and Harry Curtis found out about it, and he came to Medwell to blackmail the Admiral.

It was all rubbish about his not being able to climb out of a window, an old sea-dog like him. Everybody in the Chestnut Horse had seen him digging in his garden, and somebody claimed to have seen him on an exercise bicycle.

Mrs Cora Smith said that nothing had led her to suspect that her cousin Harry Curtis was a blackmailer.

Dan wondered if he had discovered the identity of the person who had shared the graveyard with him. He hoped not. He rather liked Admiral Jenkyn, with his ruddy cheeks and mop of white hair and quarterdeck manner. The Admiral always re-fused to employ Dan, and said why, and laughed while he was saying it.

'The plot thickens,' said Fiona.

'Ben murksome a tidy while,' said Dan, in his deepest and treacliest voice, because it was the sort of thing Fiona expected him to say.

Fiona laughed. Well, it was better than a poke in the eye with a sharp stick, but only just.

Fiona was looking particularly marvellous. She was wearing jeans and a loose sweater over a red-and-white checked shirt. Her soft hair had been blown wildly about by the October wind, which had given her cheeks a high colour like that of a ripening Worcester apple. She was on a bicycle, a better bicycle than Dan's. The season for tennis and swimming was over; the Muspratts kept no horses; Fiona got her weekend exercise, some of it, on this bicycle. Its appearance had made their meetings more frequent but more exhausting. Dan hated

71

bicycling at high speed, and to catch up with Fiona he had to lash himself along at very high speed.

His trip to the rendezvous, at least, had been leisurely.

Dotted along the hedgerows had been dunnocks, little barred browny birds with slate-grey heads and necks, usually as inconspicuous as Dan himself but now ostentatious and vainglorious, squeaking like mice at Dan and at one another. They were in twos and threes, and there were many battles. Those were males, unconvincingly fighting, laying claim to territory or ladies. It seemed to Dan that the dunnocks were pairing off, already, for the following spring; or perhaps the males wanted to spend the months of cold with somebody they could snuggle up to. Dan's father had called them 'shuffle-wings', because of the way they went about flirting with the females. A pair had once nested in a cauliflower in Dan's mother's garden, partly because, no doubt, their favourite dinner was the insects that lived in the moist shadow of the vegetables. That pair had laid two clutches, five and then four, beautiful sky-blue eggs, and every chick had survived. Rats and stoats and weasels were not permitted in Dan's mother's garden. Dan sighed at the memory of his mother in those days, as active and sun-browned as himself; he sighed at the thought of her physical pain, which she never admitted to, and the greater pain which was his betrayal of her ambitions for him, which she also never admitted to but which hit him all the time like a bolt of electricity.

Fiona had bicycled much faster, so that she was pink and panting and wind-blown and adorable, and when she laughed at Dan's rural performance it was breathless laughter.

Dan said suddenly, in his other voice, 'I wish you'd kiss me on the nose again.'

'We haven't been having dinner,' said Fiona, as though this were a reason for not kissing somebody. She added, 'We're not in a car. It's not dark.'

She then kissed him on the nose.

Dan tried to embrace her, his arms round her back, but she pushed him away with a kind of imperious gentleness.

'That's enough,' she said.

'Nay,' said Dan.

They sat side by side on a hunt jump interrupting a barbed-wire fence, and Dan put his arm round her waist. She looked for a moment as though she was going to object.

'No,' she said, not referring to his arm, but continuing the earlier conversation as though nothing had happened in between. 'The plot wasn't thick enough before. It was obvious who did the murder, and now it isn't obvious any more.'

No, it was no longer obvious to anybody who had not been between the church and the Chestnut Horse on the night of the murder.

'And now,' said Fiona, 'it's less obvious still. They picked up a tramp.'

'Vanishing breed,' said Dan. 'My mother used to say she had tramps the way other people had mice.'

'They must have been sure of a welcome,' said Fiona. 'They must have had a sign on the garden gate.'

'Never was much of a gate,' said Dan. 'What tramp? Why have the bluebottles picked him up? And how do you know about it?'

'My father was a policeman once,' said Fiona. 'In Guyana. So he's got friendly with the Detective Chief Superintendent here. So they came to dinner last night.'

'Gum,' said Dan. 'Ye ben keepen right rum comp'ny.'

'He told us about it. It wasn't a secret. It couldn't have been, because so many people were about when it happened.'

'Often the way,' said Dan. 'No decencies left.'

'He tried to sell something in a jeweller's in Milchester. It was a watch. It was American. He said he picked it up in the garden of that cottage next door to the pub.'

'Vince Mellins,' said Dan. 'Doubt if he'd have an American watch.'

'He says he picked it up there the night that man was murdered. He didn't know about the murder. He didn't know there'd been a murder. He says he never sees anybody or reads a newspaper. He says he can't read, anyway.'

'Loquacious fellow, though,' said Dan. 'Full of gab. Oratory in the Police Station.'

'Shut up,' said Fiona. 'You're the one who talks too much.'

'Not usually,' said Dan. 'You've unlocked something inside me.'

73

'Well, lock it up again, for goodness' sake. They think what he says must be true, or he wouldn't have tried to sell it so close to the place.'

'Might be brazen,' said Dan. 'Might be double bluff. Was it Harry Curtis's watch?'

'Cora Smith says not. She's never seen it. The Hedges have never seen it. It's a man's watch, anyway, a big heavy one on a metal strap. The Super says it's flashy but not very expensive.'

'"The Super",' quoted Dan. 'Almost Christian-name terms. A big, cheap, flashy watch sounds like Harry Curtis.'

'Yes, but Cora Smith had never seen it, and nobody else remembers seeing him wear it.'

'Was he wearing a watch when he was killed?'

'I've no idea. That's a good question. The police must know.'

'Maybe he was, but Debbie Chandler or Ted Goldingham pinched it before they got there.'

'Robbing the dead. What a horrible idea.'

'No worse than robbing the living, which Ted Goldingham does every day . . . If your tramp's story is true, how did a watch like that get into Vince Mellins's garden? I wonder how long it had been there. Is it waterproof? And was it going when he found it?'

'Those are more good questions,' said Fiona after a moment. 'I don't know the answer to either. I don't suppose the tramp would know if it was going or not, if he can't read. I don't suppose he knew how to wind it, so it wouldn't have been going by the time he tried to sell it.'

'Admiral Jenkyn was in America . . .'

'Neither of them had ever seen it. He always carries a gold pocket-watch.'

'So he does. But maybe not when climbing over the coal-shed . . .'

'Anyway, that's what I came to tell you,' said Fiona.

She jumped off the tiger-trap fence, and picked up her bicycle from the grassy verge of the road. Helpless, Dan followed her, and picked up his own bicycle. They stood together, two bicycles between them. Thus protected, Fiona kissed Dan on the nose. In a moment she was gone, pedalling vigorously, her hair flying, strong and slender and intelligent and the intimate friend of the Chief Detective Superintendent.

The plot had not done thickening.

A police car bonged to a halt outside Dan's cottage next morning, as he was coming out to feed his bantams.

A Detective Sergeant, known to Dan of old, said that Dan had been seen lurking outside the Chestnut Horse between ten and ten-thirty on the night of the murder.

6

It was the tramp.

His name was Snowy Burden. It may have been John or Tom or Frank thirty or fifty years before, but as far as he remembered it was Snowy. He came originally from somewhere or other. He had had a mother, presumably also called Burden, but as far as he knew no father. They had put him into somewhere, when he was quite a nipper, but he had run away. He went for a soldier at the beginning of what they called the war, liking the notion of regular rations, but they turned him down because of his tubes.

He was known to the police, who regarded him as a harmless nuisance. He had been inside a few times, for a few days at a time, not so much because he had committed dreadful crimes as because kindly magistrates had wanted to guarantee him a roof over his head in the coldest weather.

Even in the bar of the Chestnut Horse it was admitted that Snowy would not have done a bloody murder, stolen a distinctive watch, and then tried to flog the watch a few miles away a few days later.

Snowy had been resting in the garden of a house next door to the pub. It was a good place to rest in fine weather, well known to him – quiet, dark, soft to lie, and the weeds gave you shelter from the wind. He came awake to find that it was dark. That was fine. He knew he could find a place for his proper sleep in the outhouses of the pub, but only after the folk went to their beds. You could always find a bite to eat, too, outside the back door of a pub. It was sinful, all that waste. No reason the rats should have it all.

Woken, but waiting for bed, Snowy had seemingly squatted among the weeds like a garden gnome undestroyed by a natural disaster. It was thenabouts that his hand had lit on something hard – small and smooth and hard, with floppety bits at the sides. A watch, with metal straps. He put it in his pocket, the one that didn't have any holes. He should have taken it to the police? Nobody never told him about that. Was the watch going? Snowy couldn't say.

And it was thenabouts that he saw the other bloke, hiding under the trees by the wall of the churchyard. Snowy could see very well in the dark, owing to the life he led. He couldn't see to read, or to tell the time, but he could see another bloke in the dark.

Describe the bloke? That took a bit of time, a lot of patience and gentleness on the part of the police. Describing a bloke was not a thing that Snowy had ever before attempted. It came out in the end, so reducing the number of photographs Snowy had to be shown. It came out as Dan Mallett, even before they started bringing out photographs.

Nothing could surprise anybody less, than that Dan Mallett should be loitering with intent at a late hour on the night of a murder.

'I knowed 'twas 'nother bloke, some 'eres by,' said Dan to the Detective Sergeant.

'Ay, Snowy Burden,' said the Sergeant.

'Nay, in ol' trees, t'churchy-yard,' said Dan. 'Churchyard,' he amended, realising that 'churchy-yard' was over the top, and likely to jeopardise the credibility of anything else he said.

Snowy Burden had not seen any other person – only Dan, whom he identified with confidence from a photograph.

It was obvious to the police that Dan had not, in fact, murdered Mr Harry Curtis, because if he had he would have stolen something. Mr Curtis had a watch and some money and some travellers' cheques and two pieces of new lightweight luggage; according to Mrs Cora Smith nothing that she knew of was missing. If Dan had done the murder he would have nicked *something*. These were unusual grounds for not suspecting somebody of murder, but they were convincing.

Dan was called upon to explain why he had been loitering, late at night, at the edge of the churchyard. Dan tried on them that he was bird-watching (for owls); that he was moved to solitary prayer by the Service of Induction; and – least credible – that he was hoping for another sight of a pretty girl.

Like Snowy Burden, like Admiral Jenkyn, Dan had to remain on the outer fringe of the circle of suspects. Unfortunately there were no inner fringes. The centre of the circle was empty.

It was obvious to Dan that Snowy Burden had not woken up, or had gone back to sleep, when Terence Barclay came out of the pub and when Sandra Hedges came out of the pub. Either that, or he was keeping quiet out of the kindness of his heart, or he was blackmailing Terence Barclay or Sandra Hedges or both. Dan doubted if Snowy had the sophistication to blackmail anybody.

The Detective Sergeant said that Dan had been seen at the Service of Induction, and that nothing, after that, had the power to surprise the Sergeant. Dan grinned oafishly. Dan was told not to go anywhere, but to keep himself available for questioning. He tried to look as though he did not know what 'questioning' meant. The interview ended on an unsatisfactory note, but at least Dan was still, for the time being, at liberty.

Mrs Cora Smith was staying at The Brambles at the suggestion of almost everybody in a position to make any suggestion in the matter. It was, locally, much the best place for her to stay. Amy Crate, her landlady, had four outstanding merits: she was clean, honest, deaf and incurious. She was a born-again television viewer, for whom the meaningful part of the day began in the middle of the morning and ended at midnight. Early in the morning she shopped, cooked and cleaned, charging moderately when she was doing these things for a guest.

Amy had been widowed young. She was childless. Her empty life had been filled by the Tube. She was not reckoned eccentric in the village, because many children and retired men (fewer women) shared her obsession. She spoke freely of Mrs Cora Smith in the post office, but what she said added nothing to what everybody knew. Cora Smith was a shadow (sweetly pretty) on the edge of Amy Crate's consciousness, far less immediate than Sue Ellen or that naughty girl in Whatsitsname.

It was obvious to Dan (though nobody came out and told him so) that Cora Smith could not leave the country until the murder was cleared up, but that she could have gone to London or John o'Groats as long as the police knew where she was. It was obvious that anybody else would have done so, after the horror of that night. It was obvious that she didn't go because she had a good reason for staying, and the reason had a roguish grey moustache and an eye for the girls.

It was presumably costing Terence Barclay a bit of money, but that was all right because he had a bit of money. He was getting what he was paying for, which was Cora Smith, and Cora's silence about the doings of the night of the murder.

Everybody in the Chestnut Horse was still talking about the impossible coincidence – everybody coming all the way from Nebraska and finishing up in Medwell. Dan knew they were right. But there was another coincidence too strange to be believed: Terence Barclay and Sandra Hedges both creeping in and out of the alleyway beside the Chestnut Horse, furtive, in the dark, on the night of the murder. Cora Smith was by far the most credible reason – the only credible reason – for Terence Barclay being there, and both common sense and the timetable insisted that he had nothing to do with the murder. But something stank. At least something might be made to seem to stink, which might help Sandra Hedges.

Harry Curtis was *there* when Terence Barclay came a-wooing. So he threatened to blackmail Terence Barclay, so Terence Barclay stabbed him with a knife that happened to be handy. It hadn't happened like that, but it ought to have happened like that.

The preparation of the new Vicarage for the new Vicar – details of which were intimately known to those most interested, those marginally interested, and those not interested at all – ran into difficulties. These were predictable, and had been predicted, in the bar of the Chestnut Horse as elsewhere. But not by Sandra Hedges.

The Milchester Diocesan Finance Committee had acquired the new Vicarage, and was responsible for the renovations. It was bound by its own rules. Competitive tenders had been invited, from builders, plumbers, heating engineers, electricians and decorators, and low price had to be balanced against the probability of satisfactory work, and vice versa, by a committee which included a broad spectrum of opinion, preconception and sense of priority. Decisions were slow to come, slower to implement. Observers were driven to the conclusion that the smaller the problem, the greater the delay in solving it. Hands in the village were rubbed in gloomy satisfaction. People said they had known how it would be. The people they said it to had known also, and had said so. There was rare unanimity, among the women in the post office and the men in the Chestnut Horse.

The Hedges continued to stay with the Jenkyns, an arrangement which had better be satisfactory because it had no foreseeable end. It was hard on the Hedges; perhaps it was hard on the Jenkyns too. It was hard on Mrs Hedges. She was pretty and gentle and becoming more popular than any Vicar's wife in living memory. (Actually there was only one other Vicar's wife in living memory, and she had not been popular at all.) Her accent, or variations on it, was familiar to the village from the television; it was closer to the leisurely local burr than was the yacky, yuppy London sound that came out of the crimson mouths of the insurance brokers' wives who had taken over the prettier cottages in the village. Mrs Hedges seemed more interested in everybody than most of them had any right to expect. It was sad, therefore, that she seemed sometimes so gloomy. Some said she had a 'hunted' look; some said she had a 'haunted' look. It was put down, in equal measure, to the effect of Mrs Jenkyn, to not having a home of her own, and to the shock of a fellow-countryman being murdered almost on what was to be her doorstep.

Dan, who heard all three theories in the Chestnut Horse, thanked God that he was the only person who knew the reason for the look on Mrs Hedges' face. Except for the other watcher in the churchyard, the one who wasn't Snowy Burden.

It couldn't last, Dan thought. Whatever had made Mrs Hedges kill Harry Curtis would come to light by and by. You caught murderers by their motive. Sometimes you caught them because they confessed, but it seemed Mrs Hedges was not going to do that. Sometimes you caught them by means of information laid, but it seemed the other watcher was not laying any, and Dan was not going to lay any, and Snowy Burden didn't have any. Motive was what would get her, and Dan was very sorry for her future and for her present.

He shared this sorrow with his dogs, but not with Fiona Muspratt.

Fiona knew that Dan knew more than he was telling her. No eyes so guileless could be without guile. She did not think he had murdered Harry Curtis, although she thought that under extreme circumstances he would be capable of murder. She thought that she herself, under extreme circumstances, would murder to save somebody she was fond of. She knew exactly what Dan's intentions were in regard to herself. The idea made her laugh. She did not take it seriously, but it did not make her recoil. She knew she was desirable, not from self-examination but because she had been desired before. Sometimes she had desired right back at the man. She did not feel great guilt about such episodes, except for lying to her parents; she did not think that the God she believed in was a prig – Christ's first miracle was changing some water into wine, when the wine ran out at a country wedding. Nothing would come of her flirtation with Dan, if that was what it was. Meanwhile he made her laugh.

Captain Muspratt knew that Fiona knew more than she was telling them. He trusted his daughter's kindness but not her wisdom. Her kindness might lead her into doing something really silly; it had happened before. It might lead her into getting herself into serious trouble, which had bloody nearly happened before.

She was seeing somebody new. That was what they said – 'Have you got a new boyfriend?' 'Well, I'm seeing somebody.' She 'saw' somebody in the churchyard on the night of that murder, between the Vestry and the porch: her story about some yokel asking about the pointing of the psalms was belied by her excited giggle.

There was no point in trying to cross-examine her. Anything like that would be counterproductive. His years as a policemen in the colonies had made him at once suspicious and deliberately blinkered. You developed a nose which sniffed out, like a truffle-hound, the currency fiddles of certain Chinese businessmen; and experience taught you that any investigation would be courteously and absolutely blocked. Fiona might not be – often was not – as consistently and maddeningly courteous as a Chinese import-export merchant, but she would sure as hell block any research into her new boyfriend.

Joanna Muspratt said she hoped Fiona would bring the man to supper. Tony Muspratt said that if he was presentable she would already have presented him. They were filled with gloomy forebodings about gypsies or married men.

Taxed not by her father but by her mother about the new man in her life, Fiona simply laughed. The thought of him made her laugh. Her parents did not know what to make of that.

Dan knew that Fiona Muspratt and her parents were dining on Saturday with Sir George and Lady Simpson. Lady Simpson told him about it on Tuesday, and she told him again on Friday. She amused herself with the notion that Dan might come, to amuse Fiona; it was a joke with herself, which she knew Dan to be incapable of understanding.

Of course Sir George would amuse Fiona, said Lady Simpson, and so would Terence Barclay. Mr Barclay amused everybody. That was on Tuesday. On Friday the news was different. No Barclays to dinner, others instead. Terence Barclay had a previous engagement, unknown to Monica Barclay; or something pressing had come up.

Dan made uncouth rural noises at the back of his throat, reacting to these tidings of aristocratic social life.

Terence Barclay, almost at the last moment, had cried off dinner with the grandest of the local nobs – had cried off a party at which Fiona was to be present. Business? On Saturday evening? It was possible (Dan himself often had business on a Saturday evening) but it was grossly improbable.

A pressing engagement? It was pressing all right, and Dan knew who was doing the pressing. He thought he would make a detour, on Saturday night, by way of the cottage where Cora Smith was living.

'I've been in Britain for fifteen months,' said Sandra Hedges, 'and married for more than a year, and still I come up against surprises every day.'

'You're lucky,' said Fiona Muspratt. 'I've only come up against one since we moved here.'

It was after dinner, the two of them on a window-seat. There were two other couples both in age between the Muspratts (middle fifties) and the Simpsons (geriatric); there were the new Vicar and his wife, released for the evening from the Jenkyns; and there was a young man for Fiona. He was all right, but he was still in the dining-room with the men and the port and the conversation about politics.

The young man was not so very young. He was about thirty (a little younger than Dan, Fiona thought); he was called Francis Morley; he had been in the cavalry but was now in the City; he was a kind of cousin of Lady Simpson's, and was staying in the house. He had never been married but twice engaged – once the girl had broken it off and once he, full of horror, had had to break it off, which Fiona heard not from him but from Lady Simpson, before dinner. He was a tall and sufficiently handsome young man with smooth fair hair and gentle manners. She thought she was looking pretty good, and he showed at dinner that he thought so, too. He told her that he did not play bridge – that, at any rate, he would not do so that evening. She smiled in response to the implied compliment, and he smiled in response to her smile. Fiona's mother looked at Francis Morley with approval.

After dinner, it seemed to Fiona that she and Sandra Hedges, with tacit and simultaneous agreement, homed on the window-seat in the drawing-room. Fiona had her first extended, one-to-one conversation with Sandra Hedges. They compared

Continental travel notes and impressions of the village. They compared experiences of living in such a village, which Fiona had never done before and which she had been doing only a little longer than Sandra.

'I'm more of an outsider here than you are,' said Fiona. 'Though you come from so far away you've got a ready-made slot to fit into.'

'Aren't there any kids of your age?'

'In Milchester, yes. In the village you're the youngest person I've talked to since we came here.'

'It's kind of isolated. I guess they move away.'

'They have to, if they want jobs. But I got fed up with London.'

'There must be somebody who lives here who amuses you.'

'You and your husband do. I can't think of anybody else. Well,' Fiona amended, as cocks crowed in her brain, 'only one person. He amuses me all right. But my mother would have a fit if I asked him to supper.'

Sandra laughed sympathetically, conveying the notion that she, too, had had a friend whom she could not possibly ask to her family's home for supper. A kind of greyness came into her face, on the heels of the laugh, conveying the notion that the memory of that person was hideous to Sandra.

It was inevitable that one of the quacking ladies should start to quack about the local murder; no local party was complete without the subject. The ladies paraded the latest news, as revealed by their cleaning-women, to an audience who already knew it, from their cleaning-women. The conversation was so inevitable, so predictable, that it was hardly a coincidence that it overlapped Sandra's laugh of sympathy and her grey look of remembered terror.

Fiona remembered the moment in the Service of Induction.

'Dan Mallett was prowling round outside the pub that night,' said a woman who looked like a wrestler designed by a committee.

'Dear Dan,' said Lady Simpson. 'Sometimes I hardly understand what he says.'

'He was spotted by the tramp who found that mysterious watch. You'll never believe why he said he was there.'

The other ladies would believe it, because they had already heard it, but this was not going to stop the wrestler.

'He was hoping to glimpse a girl!'

'He has a dreadful reputation with girls,' said Lady Simpson, 'and I can understand it all too well. Those great innocent blue eyes!'

They all laughed. They were being tolerant and grown-up.

Fiona felt herself blushing. She knew with certainty that the story was true, and that it was herself Dan had been hoping to see. She found that she felt enormously pleased.

'But he says he didn't see the murderer,' said the wrestler. 'My Lily says she heard that from Mrs Gundry.'

The policeman's wife. Everybody else's daily had heard it too, from the same source, together with PC Gundry's conviction that Dan had done it, being the biggest villain unhung.

Fiona glanced from the speaker to Sandra Hedges, wondering if her blush had been perceived, if the reason for it was obvious.

She was chilled by what she saw. In Sandra's face was not the greyness of remembered terror, but the pallor of living death.

Suddenly Fiona knew that the face of Harry Curtis had blasted the happiness out of Sandra's face, there in the Service of Induction; that the brief conversation in the Church Rooms, which everybody knew about, was not the formal, conventional nothing she had reported; that he was the man in Sandra's past whom she could not ask to her home.

Fiona knew that Sandra Hedges had murdered Harry Curtis, and that Dan had seen her coming away from the pub.

Dan woke up at noon on Sunday, as he had told himself to do.

He had been up much earlier, at seven-thirty, to feed and pamper his dogs, birds and mother. Looking after the dogs and birds was easy, a matter of routine in which they co-operated with goodwill. Looking after his mother was complex and protracted; it was possible to get a little food into her, but impossible to placate her. He had had only two hours' sleep.

He had had an exhausting but not unprofitable night.

He set off for the Medwell Court preserves: they were for the time being unkeepered, which meant fewer birds but fewer interruptions. He chose a route which, on foot, took him by a moderate detour past The Brambles, where Amy Crate watched her television and Cora Smith, from time to time, laid her pretty kittenish head.

The cottage was dark, except for one curtained window which emitted splinters of bluish light: Amy's TV. Being deaf, Amy had it turned up high: from outside the garden Dan could hear the yap of voices and the surge of studio laughter.

If Cora Smith was here, she was upstairs in bed in the dark. If not, she was somewhere else.

Dan had time on his hands. He had most of the hours of darkness. It was not cold. He crept up to Amy Crate's sitting-room window, and watched the television over her shoulder. An infrequent viewer, he was fascinated and repelled by what he saw, which was a crowd of garish people talking to one another amid gales of applause. He was sure that he would hear anybody coming or going, in spite of the big square eye and the maniac noise.

He watched the rest of the programme, and the next one, marvelling at the multicoloured lushness of the commercials and wondering to whom they were addressed. Somebody was shooting at somebody (this was in a police thriller, not in the chat show) when he heard a car go slowly by in the lane. It stopped twenty yards beyond the garden gate. Dan crossed the patch of lawn, and peeped through the scraggy privet of the hedge. He could see only the rear lights of the car, twice as bright as normal because the brakes were on, hiding behind their crimson radiance anything beyond. A door slammed, and somebody emerged into the glow of the lights. The car immediately drove away.

The figure on foot was a woman. It was Cora Smith. There was no knowing who was in the car, but there was no doubting who it was.

Dan nestled in the privet like a young yellowhammer, watching Cora Smith walk to the cottage and let herself in. After a moment a light came on upstairs. Cora had not stopped to talk to Amy Crate. Probably she was tired, rumpled, and laden with banknotes.

Dan wondered how Monica Barclay had stood it all those years. He guessed that other people had wondered the same thing.

He went softly on his way to Medwell Court, and began laying his 'angles'.

He picked up a number of birds in the first light of dawn. Chilly it was now, with mist sitting on the water-meadows like a poultice. It was a bit early to be taking pheasants; legally, the season to shoot them had started, but some of the young cocks had scarcely grown tails. Dan let these babies go. They trotted off into the undergrowth disdainfully, in no particular hurry, as though intent to prove that they were not frightened of a little squirt like Dan.

He went home with a squishy sack, on foot, crossing the country without reference to where the roads happened to be. There were two or three places where he was sure he could get rid of the birds, including the one where he had recently paid for a fancy dinner. He arrived back just in time for the dogs, too early for the bantams, and too late for his mother.

He put her in the chair by the kitchen range, gave her the local paper, and went back to bed.

While he was asleep, Fiona came with a message.

She must have come very quietly and left very quietly, and negotiated with his mother very quietly. His mother had said, as far as Dan could gather from the scraps she threw him, that Dan was away, was not expected back, would never be back, did not live there, did not exist. Fiona had presumably gone back to her car, discouraged, and driven away. But she had left a note. Dan's mother first denied the existence of any note, then querulously searched for it, refusing Dan's assistance, and at last found it, in the pocket of the apron she uselessly wore, crowing with derisive triumph that she had found it and not himself.

Dan looked with interest at Fiona's handwriting, which he had not seen before. There was a lot about her he had not seen. He gulped a little, contemplating hidden territories. Her writing was strong and Italic, ballpoint on pale grey paper.

She asked him to meet her at Butcher's Bridge at three

o'clock that afternoon. *Urgent*, she said, underlining the word.

Not a romantic rendezvous; more a business conference.

'Wench,' said his mother, pretending not to study his face as he read the stiff little note. 'Pretty as a flower.'

'Hum,' said Dan, to whom the word was a frequent necessity.

'Too good for the likes o' you.'

'Oh yes,' said Dan. 'Not so much a friend. Associate. Ben a girt helpen han',' he added, moderating his accent towards his mother's.

'Gammon,' she said, and closed her eyes not in sleep but in rage.

They had what his mother called 'dinner', what in his years at the bank he had learned to call 'lunch', what Fiona undoubtedly called 'lunch', what Lady Simpson probably called 'luncheon'. They had a steamy mess of vegetables – cabbage, broccoli, onions, baby marrows – from various gardens where Dan pretended to work, lightly boiled and then fried, deliberately slightly under-cooked so that they gave you something to bite on, with pieces of streaky bacon like the wreckage of a ship in a swamp. Dan thought it was delicious; his mother said it was disgusting. After she had finished not eating it, she sat like a gravestone waiting for him to clear it away.

There was not enough water in the tub for the washing-up. Dan sighed – not as theatrically as his mother would have sighed – and went to the well. While he was out she screamed, not in fear but in rage.

It was a wood-mouse, what some called a field-mouse, but not quite a field-mouse because it was a long-tailed field-mouse. It was browner than a house-mouse, who was a very grey fellow, with a whiter tummy and bigger, softer eyes. Those big eyes were as misleading as Dan's own. The long-tailed wood-mouse was just as messy and greedy as any other mouse, and it only came to see them because the cottage was warmer and drier than the woods. It was a country mouse, a yokel, a simpleton, all the things that Dan spent much of his time pretending to be; it would be much easier to catch in a trap than its sophisticated, domesticated cousin. The trap was thoroughly necessary and thoroughly repugnant.

Keeping an eye on the time, Dan heated some water for the washing-up, and while he was doing so baited and set the trap by the little hole in what would have been the wainscot, if there had been a wainscot, through which their visitor had disappeared.

Maybe Mr Harry Curtis had not come from Nebraska to lime a twig but to bait a mousetrap. Dan had a bit of the rind of a Stilton; what bait would Harry Curtis have used? It had drawn the mouse to the trap, yes, by way of Vince Mellins's garden; but Harry Curtis had not reckoned on the power of despair.

Urgent, said Fiona. The water was slow heating up. He had to do the washing-up before he left the cottage, or his mother would self-conflagrate with rage. She was near doing so anyway, as she watched him shuffle apologetically out.

Dan bicycled slowly, slowly towards Butcher's Bridge, three miles away downstream. He had time to go slowly, but perhaps not as slowly as he did. In the ditches, the undergrowth had withered and fallen away, in unseasonable early frosts. In its place there were thousands of tiny green seedlings, children of the flowers of early summer. Many would survive the winter, and thrust upwards as clumps of foxglove and meadowsweet and rosebay willow-herb. Renewal, even in death. As the river looped near to Dan's road, there were sallows in the hedgerow. They were still in full leaf, but at the base of each leaf was a bright red bud, and some of the buds were already split to reveal the flower inside, the little grey mouse-like catkin. Life renewing itself while still in the vigour of life. Sandra Hedges was doing that. Would she, like a foxglove seedling, survive this winter?

Who had been in the churchyard with Dan, when Sandra Hedges came out of the Chestnut Horse?

Butcher's Bridge carried a road once economically important, now very little used. It led to quarries exhausted before the turn of the century, and a mill whose stones had not turned since the end of the First War. The bridge was two-spanned, with a massive central pillar, often sketched by the Art Club in the summer, said to have been built by Telford. Dan had always liked it, but on that sunny October Sunday afternoon it looked better than ever before.

Fiona had a high colour, from recent bicycling, which suited her very well. She had taken off the man's tweed cap she had been wearing; her soft wavy hair was wild and lovely. There was a smear of mud or grease on her temple, which had no detrimental effect at all.

She began to speak while he was dismounting. He held up a hand, as soon as he had a hand to hold up, with an imperious gesture he did not know he knew. Fiona looked as surprised as Dan felt. He pulled out his handkerchief – clean, taken fresh from his drawer when the washing-up was done. He slid round the end of the bridge's parapet, crouched by the side of the swollen water, and moistened his handkerchief. He glanced at Fiona, who was watching him with a peculiar expression. He guessed his own expression was a mite peculiar. He rejoined Fiona, holding the damp handkerchief.

'Mother never let me talk to strange men with a dirty face,' he said.

'What strange man has a dirty face?'

'Clever-clever,' said Dan. 'Lean forward.'

To his surprise she did. With one hand on the back of her head, he mopped clean the muddy temple. She suffered this, but he knew she would not suffer it for long. He kissed the place where the mud had been. She suffered this, too. He embarked on further kisses, in new areas, but she straightened and pushed him away.

'Thank you very much for the blanket-bath,' she said, 'but that isn't what I came here for.'

'Not "urgent",' admitted Dan. 'Not like putting on the brakes on the precipice.'

'That's exactly what I'm doing,' said Fiona, 'putting on the brakes on the precipice. What I want to know is, how long are you going to go on protecting Sandra Hedges?'

7

Dan gulped, speechless, as astonished as though his brakes had locked on a precipice.

Fiona stared at him, more serious than he had ever seen her. Her solemnity made her look younger, instead of older; she looked like an adorable fourteen-year-old. He knew that this was not the moment to do anything about that.

'As far as I know,' he said at last, 'it isn't Mrs Hedges who needs protecting. It was Admiral Jenkyn that crook antique dealer caught in his headlights.'

'How do you know he's a crook?'

'All antique dealers are crooks,' said Dan, thinking of the one in Milchester who never asked the provenance of the silver Dan was selling.

'Rubbish,' said Fiona. 'Never mind about that. It's not in the least proved that it was Admiral Jenkyn that man saw. In fact it's almost proved he wasn't. And why would Admiral Jenkyn murder a man he'd never seen before?'

'Of course he'd seen him before. Haven't you got your ear to the ground? Meaning the post office or the bar of the Chestnut Horse. Admiral Jenkyn went to Colorado, which is slap next door to Nebraska, which is where everybody comes from in this story.'

'He didn't go to Nebraska and he didn't meet that man Curtis and he didn't climb out of his window that night, and if he'd come out of the pub you would have seen him, because you were lurking about –'

'More loitering. Idling away the time, like they do on the boulevards of Paris.'

'Lurking about waiting to –'

'See you again. Just a glimpse at a distance. No thought of ravishment or mischief. Idea of ravishment only to be examined to be dismissed. Protected by dragons. No offence intended to your parents.'

'You're gabbling and gabbling,' said Fiona, 'so as not to answer my question. What I want to know is, what are you going to do about it?'

'Putting it another way, what are we going to do about it?'

'Me? What can I do? I wasn't there.'

'Yes.'

'Not at that time.'

'Enough to see what you saw.'

'I saw it again, last night at the Simpsons'.'

'Lady Simpson is enough to . . .' began Dan. He stopped. It was no time for jokes, in his banker's voice or any other voice.

Fiona, having dinner at the Simpsons', had seen Sandra Hedges' face when the murder was discussed, when Harry Curtis was discussed.

Fiona convinced Dan immediately. She was deeply serious. She was deeply concerned because she was kind-hearted and because she greatly liked Sandra Hedges. She was intelligent and quick-witted and perceptive. When she described what she had seen, she had to be believed. Her conclusions were something else. They might not have been believed by anybody else. Dan accepted that her theory was right because he already knew it to be right.

But he said, 'No no. Mrs Hedges went to bed when Mrs Jenkyn said she did. And there she stayed. Her husband said she did.'

'He'd protect her, obviously.'

'Not obviously at all. Ordained Minister of the Church, telling fibs to the bluebottles? Whatever next?'

He could not admit, even to Fiona, that he knew she was right. It was knowledge that could be shared with absolutely nobody. It was the only way he could help Mrs Hedges – ignorance, 'no' to all questions; he had left the churchyard and pub before anybody went in or came out.

He could share this knowledge with nobody, but he already shared it. With Mrs Hedges. And with one other. It probably wasn't Admiral Jenkyn, that other watcher in the churchyard, and it wasn't Snowy Burden. Dan had the sense of sitting on a stick of dynamite, which when it exploded would atomise not him but another. Sitting quite still was not a noble or amusing thing to do, but it was the only way he could help Sandra Hedges.

'You know I'm right but you won't admit it,' said Fiona. 'And I want to know what we're going to do about it.'

Dan was pleased by her acceptance of the plural pronoun, but displeased that she was banging on about her knowledge, so to call it, that Sandra Hedges had murdered Harry Curtis.

'Even if that were true,' said Dan, 'the answer would still be "nothing". Masterly inactivity. See no evil, et cetera.'

'You're just frightened of getting yourself into trouble,' said Fiona. 'I didn't think you'd be a coward.'

'What trouble?' said Dan. He foresaw no more trouble than usual, at least once he had disposed of the dawn's sackful of pheasants.

'I've known for ages you were keeping something back.'

'I've been keeping a lot of things back.'

'I'm not talking about *that*.'

Nor was she. Nor would she. Nor could he.

She wanted to do something active, positive, even perilous, to help Sandra Hedges. He knew there was no such thing. Dan kept his patience, but Fiona lost hers. She bicycled away, vexation lending astonishing power to her legs. Dan hoped she simmered down soon, or her calf-muscles would become over-developed.

Fiona got home to find her mother in a state of unusual dither. On the table in the hall was a large vase of carnations, which had not been there in the morning.

Francis Morely had called, just after Fiona had left. He was in his own car, a BMW. He came to see Fiona, and was keenly disappointed not to do so. Though pressed by Fiona's mother to stay for tea, he had to get straight up to London to meet some Australians. But he said he was coming back to stay with the Simpsons, soon and often.

'Soon and often,' repeated Fiona's mother.

There was nowhere in the village you could buy a bunch of

carnations on Sunday morning. Francis Morley must have made a special trip into Milchester. He was tall and good-looking and interesting; he seemed prosperous; he was a man who drove twelve miles on a Sunday morning to get a girl a bunch of expensive flowers.

It was impossible not to be highly gratified. In Fiona's mind, gratification sat on top of sympathetic misery like the cream on Irish coffee.

The Reverend Gordon Hedges was asked, apologetically, to confirm his statement, which had taken some time to make some time before. He was very patient, considering that he was trying to get round that silent and apathetic majority which had not come to the Service of Induction or the Church Rooms. He went through it all again, with what was described as a wry laugh.

Yes: his wife had left the Church Rooms, with Admiral and Mrs Jenkyn, about three-quarters of an hour before he himself left, he having felt obliged to talk to everybody who wanted to talk to him. On his way back to the Jenkyns', on foot, he had been intercepted, to be more exact followed and caught, by the lady whom he now knew to be Mrs Cora Smith, who was in some distress, but with whom his conversation must remain confidential until such time as he was asked about it in a Court of Law. When they reached the Jenkyns', he found that Mrs Jenkyn had stayed up for him. He handed Mrs Smith over to Mrs Jenkyn, who, as far as he knew, put her straight to bed. His wife was already in bed and there remained; she could not have gone out without his knowledge. He did not see Admiral Jenkyn until the morning. He did not see Mrs Jenkyn after she had gone away with Mrs Smith. It was impossible, from the positions of the bedrooms, for Mrs Smith to have gone out without his knowledge, unless she did so at two-thirty in the morning, until which hour Gordon Hedges lay wakeful in bed, stimulated by what were for him and his wife the momentous events of that day.

It was in theory possible for Admiral Jenkyn, whose window was on the other side of the house, to have left and returned, by the window, without Mr Hedges' knowledge; this on the assumption that the Admiral was physically capable of climbing in and out of his bedroom by a window and the roof of an outhouse. It was, by the same token, theoretically possible that Mrs Jenkyn had gone out and come in again.

Lady Simpson was one of many local notables who had been to the Jenkyns' house; she was one of the few who had been upstairs in it. As though to prove this, she gave Dan, on Monday afternoon, a detailed account of the upstairs rooms, their use, decoration, and outlook. Dan did not require this information, since he had been there too, but he got it whether he wanted it or not. It was marginally more restful to listen to Lady Simpson than to dig her herbaceous border. In any case, Dan's reasons for exploring the Jenkyns' bedrooms would not have been understood by Lady Simpson. He had not in the event taken anything; he had pocketed a silver button-hook from the dressing-table in the spare bedroom, his fingers guided by habit rather than brain, but he had returned it; he had no use for a button-hook, and he did not think the studiously un-inquisitive proprietor of The Box of Delights in Milchester would much want it either.

Lady Simpson's theory was one Dan had already heard, in the post office during the morning and in the Chestnut Horse at noon. Mrs Jenkyn had heard the Admiral go out. She knew that he was in trouble with a man from Nebraska, deriving from the time he went to Colorado, and she was afraid of what he might do. She crept out after the Admiral and followed him. Now she was protecting him.

Lady Simpson had read more mystery stories than the women in the post office, although she had seen less television; she knew as well as they did what you did when somebody blackmailed you. If you were an Admiral you had a commando dagger. After the murder, you left it behind, having put the victim's fingerprints on it. It was difficult to blame the Admiral. Being blackmailed must be a nasty experience. Expensive, too, and Admiral Jenkyn didn't have much besides his pension.

There was a minority which continued to believe that Dan had done it; this view was almost, though not quite, expressed in his presence. But the majority decision was that the Admiral had done it, and good luck to him.

Admiral Jenkyn continued to deny that he had climbed out of any window, could climb out of his bedroom window, had ever been to Nebraska, had ever met Harry Curtis unless he had had two words with him in the Church Rooms. Mrs Jenkyn admitted that, if threatened by fire, she could probably climb out of her bedroom window, but denied that she had done so. 'They would, wouldn't they?' said the village.

'Dwindling minority,' said Dan to Fiona, 'people who weren't loitering outside the pub when that bloke got murdered.'

'How can you possibly think Mrs Jenkyn had anything to do with it?'

'Tigress defending her whelp.'

'Her whelp's in New Zealand.'

'So he is. That means Mrs Jenkyn was tucked up safe in bed all night.'

He supposed there must be grounds for supposing that Mrs Jenkyn had crept out. She would hardly be suspected of doing so simply because nobody had seen her not doing so. In that case, half the countryside would be suspected.

Dan hoped half the countryside was suspected; it would take people's eyes off the person who had actually done it.

Dan continued to pretend to disbelieve Fiona's theory about the murder.

Old Madge Beard went to the police; all on her own, except for the thirty women following her and urging her on; she rang the bell of Jim Gundry's cottage, and in she went and got it off her chest.

Everybody knew what she was going to say, because she had told them all before she went. They said she must go to Jim Gundry. She said she'd always kept herself respectable.

'I niver 'ad no dealens,' she said.

She had kept quiet before because she hadn't properly understood about Admiral Jenkyn and the American. She didn't hold with Admirals or Americans or murdering or the police, but people kept on and on about it in the post office, and in the finish even Madge understood that Admiral Jenkyn had said he didn't properly talk to that American.

Madge had been to church, not properly knowing what she was letting herself in for. A Service of Induction sounded like something quite different. She didn't know what they were on about. She didn't understand the general invitation to the Church Rooms, but she followed the crowd. She spilled something hot on herself. She went off into a corner to mop herself up, and there, hidden from the rest of the party, was Admiral Jenkyn talking to a stranger. She never talked to Admiral Jenkyn herself, then or any other time; she never could understand what people of that sort were saying. But she knew him by sight.

The stranger? Description was beyond Madge Beard's powers, but she conveyed a big bloke in a funny coat. There were plenty of big blokes in the Church Rooms, but not many funny coats. There was no doubt in anybody's mind that the Admiral had been talking to Harry Curtis, in a corner, out of earshot of anybody, out of sight of anybody except Madge Beard. Quite a long talk they had, very serious. PC Gundry rendered it 'earnest' in his report.

Madge Beard was bought two brown ales in the Chestnut Horse, and she went to sleep at the bar.

Admiral Jenkyn said, to the police and everybody else, that if he had spoken to the American he had forgotten about it. He thought his word should be accepted over that of a drunken and dirty old woman. It was generally admitted that Madge Beard could do with a scrub, but it was held that she wouldn't have – probably couldn't have – invented the scene she described. There was nothing in it for her, except two brown ales.

The division in the village, which survived from medieval times, was made sharper and deeper by these events.

There were two camps, the higher smaller, the lower larger.

They had changed in relation to one another, within living memory, owing to the new affluence of the larger and lower camp, which had videos and washing machines, and the greater size of the smaller and higher camp with its immigrants from London. As everywhere else in England, the diagnostic difference was in language, both accent and vocabulary. As soon as anybody opened his mouth, you knew to which camp he belonged.

There were people to be seen in the village, to be sure, who occupied neither camp, or took a stand in the no man's land between the camps – outsiders all – like the Milchester vet who came to look at people's ponies, the Milchester wine-merchant who came out with telephone orders in his Volvo estate, the Milchester estate agent who sold cottages for conversion to weekend retreats for insurance brokers. Probably in their own places they were as securely encamped as in the village were Sir George Simpson and his guests on the one hand, and Dan's mother and old Curly Godden on the other. Nobody escaped. That Mrs Ponder-Parker who had bought Cresset Cottage a year before, she declared her allegiance the moment she arrived, by giving a house-warming with champagne cocktails, employing Dan Mallett in her garden, and wearing a fur tippet to church. She was exposed pretty briskly, by both sides. On the opposite side there was young Dennis Weaver, who dropped out of college and set himself up as a self-employed painter and decorator. Nobody was fooled by his old van and his overalls.

Dan was unique, at least in that village, in his ability to jump from one world to another. He found that his terminology automatically changed with his clothes and accent. It sometimes occurred to him to wonder who and what he was – a yokel pretending to be an Assistant Bank Manager, or the other way about? His dual personality sharpened rather than blurred the clarity of the distinction.

So did the murder, and the theories about the murder. The nobs stood firm for Admiral and Mrs Jenkyn; though they might have had private doubts, in public they closed ranks in defence of one of their own. The villagers were not censorious, precisely – they just knew the Admiral had done it. Knowing why, they understood that he had to do it. He would cop it in the end, in spite of his wife's loyal evidence, because something would be dug up about his meeting with Harry Curtis, twenty years before, in Colorado or Nebraska. Those American cops were pretty tough, as you could tell by the television serials. The village sat back and waited for news from Omaha. All that divided the bar in the Chestnut Horse was a difference as to the pronunciation of 'Omaha', and an abiding minority conviction that Dan had done it.

Mrs Cora Smith was declared a member of the upper camp; although her accent and choice of words were strange, her very strangeness made her immune from classification, until she was classified by the nobs as one of themselves. It was not certain where the late Harry Curtis would have gone, supposing that he had stayed alive and stayed in the village. The jacket he wore to church would not have been worn by Sir George Simpson or Mr Edwin Calloway; on the other hand, his new lightweight luggage would not have been owned by Ted Goldingham. Perhaps he would have been on a par with the wine merchant from Milchester, who wore a pale plastic jacket with bands of colour on the sleeves.

Dan pondered these matters, as he bicycled slowly home in the autumn dusk. He was dressed to occupy the very bottom position on the village social scale, even to binder-twine round his baggy corduroy trousers, tying them in needless nooses below the knee. His appearance was as parodic as the voice that went with it. He was not sure which made Fiona Muspratt laugh harder. He was, in a way, fed up with her mirth, although she seemed inexhaustibly devoted to it. It had started by bringing them together; now it held them apart.

He wondered what he would do if Admiral Jenkyn were arrested for the murder of Harry Curtis.

Mr and Mrs Charles Black came back from their holiday in Majorca, to be told by some thirty people, on the day of their return, all that all of the thirty knew about the murder. The facts thus presented were broadly the same, although the appended theories, offered as facts but distinguishable from them, differed according to the social level of the speaker.

It was all of particular interest to Mr and Mrs Black, because they had left the village on the very evening of the murder. They had said they were going to leave that evening, and they did. They went to the Service of Induction; they went for as long as they could to the party in the Church Rooms; and then their son-in-law Roland drove them to Heathrow. It was not a convenient time to catch an aeroplane, but it was what their package stipulated. Their daughter Helen and her husband were house-sitting and dog-sitting while they were away. This was an arrangement normal in the vicinity, suiting all parties. It suited the Blacks, because they saved the cost of kennels and reduced the risk of burglary, except by their son-in-law, whom they tried to trust. It suited Roland Harris because the whisky was free and he preferred living in Medwell to living in Peckham. It suited Helen, because it gave her a cleaning-woman twice a week and a gardener at unpredictable times. (The gardener was Dan Mallett.) The young Harrises had not been to the Service of Induction or the party in the Church Rooms; the baby was the public and most respectable reason, generally accepted, for this omission.

It was established that the Blacks had left the Church Rooms at least three-quarters of an hour, perhaps an hour and a half, before the murder, that they had gone straight home to pick up their luggage, tickets and passports, and that they had driven to Heathrow, where Roland Harris had seen them into the Departure Lounge. All this was known at once to all classes, by way of PC Gundry, the Chestnut Horse, the post office, daily cleaning-women, and other normal sources. It was accepted that the Blacks could have had nothing to do with the murder, which was generally if tacitly regretted, the Blacks being members of that awkward stratum which was asked to drinks by Sir George and Lady Simpson but not to dinner.

The Blacks were questioned by the police, since they had been to the service and to the Church Rooms. Had they seen anything relevant? They hardly knew. Had they seen the late Harry Curtis? They had seen a big, grey-haired man, unknown to them, in a checked coat of a kind which they had seen in Majorca but which they had never seen in the village. The police believed, and the Blacks agreed, that it was Harry Curtis they had seen. In church? No; they had sat at the back, in order to avoid the bottleneck of people leaving; they were not so accustomed to flying that they checked in less than two hours before their flight-time. In the Church Rooms? Yes, they remembered seeing him there because they were surprised to see him there. Violet Black had passed a remark about that coat, to which Charles had replied with a non-committal grunt.

They remembered seeing the stranger in conversation with Sir George Simpson.

No word of the conversation was heard by either of the Blacks, owing to the noise in the Church Rooms, but they both saw it, and independently described, in identical terms, the manner of the two men. The conversation had been 'earnest', the word used by PC Gundry, though not by Madge Beard, in the former's transcription of the latter's description of the conversation between Harry Curtis and Admiral Jenkyn.

This was known to the public almost as soon as it was known to the police. The Blacks had felt cheated, knowing that they were practically airborne when the murder was committed; they were not apt to be modest about the bombshell they brought back in their luggage.

Sir George Simpson at first roundly denied that he had exchanged so much as a word with the stranger, though he admitted (as he had previously admitted) seeing the man in the odd check coat. This was embarrassing, as a categorical statement to the opposite effect had been made by a couple who were on drinking, if not dining, terms with his wife and himself. Driven most respectfully into a corner, Sir George allowed that he could not swear, with his hand on the Bible, that he had not addressed a remark to, or been addressed by, the American. But he maintained that the conversation, if indeed there had been one, was brief, conventional, forgettable and forgotten. An 'earnest' conversation of any length he continued vehemently to deny.

This was not at all like the disagreement of Admiral Jenkyn and Madge Beard. The Admiral could, and did, disparage Madge Beard, dismiss her as an unclean and untrustworthy old bag. She was manifestly these things. Violet Black was both clean and credible, and it would have been both ungallant and unsafe for Sir George to have stated otherwise. One result was that Lady Simpson had to avoid Mrs Black. She stopped her car outside the post office; she saw Violet Black get out of *her* car and go in; she had to sit in the car and wait until the woman came out. It wasted a lot of time, and shortened, later in the morning, Lady Simpson's conversation with Dan Mallett.

The other result was that the police were obliged to scrutinise the possibility of a connection between Sir George Simpson and the late Harry Curtis.

The village was there before them. Everybody knew that Sir George had been in senior management in the oil industry, and that one of the things you did if you were an oil tycoon was to travel all over the world, including America. Obviously, said the regulars in the Chestnut Horse, Sir George had been to Nebraska, had it off with a tart in a motel, been seen by Harry Curtis, was being blackmailed by Curtis. 'Plain as the nose on your face,' they said.

Two lines of questioning suggested themselves. Where had Sir George been, all Harry Curtis's life? And where had he been on the night of the murder?

Of course he had been to the United States, some fifteen to eighteen times. Lady Simpson had accompanied him perhaps a third of those times. He had visited many states, he thought at least twenty. He had travelled by domestic airlines or in the company aircraft of various oil companies. He did not remember that he had ever set foot in Nebraska, but he could not swear that he had not, as it were inadvertently, stepped across the state line from Kansas or Iowa. His last visit had been twelve years previously, shortly before his retirement. Lady Simpson had not been with him. He had visited New York, Texas and California.

'Dirty old man,' said the dirty old men in the Chestnut Horse. 'Wunner what 'e got 'at tart to do to un?'

Anybody who went from New York to California, as the crow flies, was practically bound to go by way of Nebraska.

Sir George was stinking rich. Handshake, pension, investments – he was a blackmailer's dream. It was a different league from poor old Admiral Jenkyn.

Charles and Violet Black were practically ostracised by the gentry, but Violet got excellent service in the post office.

The Simpsons had no living-in servants. (Nobody had within miles; nobody had for years, since Major Marsh sold Medwell Court, unless you counted the caretakers at the Priory) They slept in separate rooms, had done for years, owing to Sir George's occasional need, which he himself deplored, for a cigarette at four in the morning. Lady Simpson had gone to bed about twenty past eleven, on the night of the murder, leaving her husband with a nightcap and a book. She had not seen him until he brought her a cup of tea, as he always did, at eight o'clock in the morning. But it was impossible that he could have gone out and come in again without her knowing. He always bolted the front door, before coming up to bed. The bolt slid home with a crash. She always lay in bed listening for that crash; she liked hearing it – it made her feel safe, and it meant that Sir George was going to bed. She heard it on that night, only a few minutes after she was in bed, her head having hardly touched the pillow. When she went down the next morning she drew back the bolt. It had been bolted; it could not have been unbolted and rebolted, not without waking her up. She was completely positive about this, because within an hour her cleaning-woman had told her about the murder, and she had gone over everything that had happened while it was still fresh in her mind.

Sir George repeated, slowly and loudly, what he had already said. He did not think he had ever been to Nebraska. He had never, there or elsewhere, met Harry Curtis. He had never been blackmailed. He had no guilty secret for which he could be blackmailed. He did not think he had spoken to Harry Curtis in the Church Rooms; if he had done so, there were few words and those without importance. After leaving the Church Rooms he had gone straight home, with his wife, and had remained in her company until she went to bed. He had followed her within minutes, not having in the meantime left his chair.

Apparently there was as much sensation in Omaha, about a Nebraskan being murdered in mysterious circumstances in a place called Medwell Fratrorum, as there would have been in the village if a Medwell man had been murdered in Nebraska. It was a thing that did not commonly happen to Nebraskans; nobody could remember any other citizen being murdered in a place with such a name. Newspapers printed agency reports, on their third or fourth pages. The case was glamorised by the reported involvement first of a British Admiral, then of a British Sir. Mrs Cora Smith lent a glamorous touch, as did Mrs Sandra Hedges. It sent cub reporters leafing through newspaper morgues.

Sir George Simpson had a bit of bad luck.

A small-town paper, the Cranston (Nebraska) *Independent-Gazette*. Issue of 20 March 1973. Report of an accident involving a cab and a police car. News because the passenger in the cab (who suffered superficial injuries, and was not hospitalised) was a distinguished visiting Englishman, Sir Geoffrey Simpson. The evening edition carried the same story, the name corrected. The victim, who was given a cup of coffee by the police matron, stated that he was in Cranston on private business. Cranston was in eastern Nebraska, an hour from Omaha and from Lincoln.

It was not a very terrible experience, but it was not a thing anybody would forget. Sir George said he had forgotten it, that he had never heard of Cranston, that he could not imagine what 'private business' could mean, that it was a clear case of mistaken identity. He was nearly sure that he had not been in America at that time.

It was established that he had flown to San Francisco on 14 March and returned from New York on 6 April. He had forgotten his movements in between. He was getting an old man. He had never kept a diary. He did not keep engagement books after the end of the year with which they dealt. It was impossible, after fourteen years, to trace his movements by way of other people's diaries or memories, airline bookings, or hotel registers.

Harry Curtis would have been twenty-two at the time. Sir George was already rich; he was a long way from home; he was alone and probably lonely.

In general the village would have forgiven Sir George, except that he had run Admiral Jenkyn into the muck.

Lady Simpson was not at home to callers, and even Dan Mallett had a lonely morning there.

8

'It's absolutely ridiculous,' said Fiona. 'It's the most idiotic thing I ever heard.' Then she said, 'Stop it. This is no time for that sort of thing.'

Dan thought there was no time that was no time for 'that sort of thing', but he did stop it because she pushed him away with her bicycle.

'They might as well go about saying Mildred Calloway did it,' said Fiona, 'because she once worked in New York.'

The idea did not immediately strike Dan, because he was distracted by the proximity of Fiona. She had her wind-blown, high-coloured look, consequence of high wind and high speed on her bicycle. Nobody had any business to look so healthy. Nobody had any business to look irresistible, and then be shoving bicycles at a person. Ravishment was unthinkable, and given Fiona's health and fitness almost certainly impossible; gentler methods were failing. Dan felt a despair which, in the many similar situations which had befallen him, was quite new to him. It made him for a moment just not care about anything else.

It was only for a moment, partly because Fiona was being very serious and everything she said was right, and partly because it was only for a moment that he could forget Sandra Hedges' face. He had felt before the emotion he identified as compassion, but never, he thought, so keenly. He was delighted, on the Vicar's wife's behalf, that a lot of other people could be suspected of the murder of Harry Curtis. The more the better. Sir George Simpson added to the confusion. Dan himself had said, even before they knew about Sir George having been in Nebraska, that a dwindling minority of the village had not been lurking or loitering in or near the churchyard on the night of the murder. It would be nice for Mrs Hedges, whom

Dan had still not met, if the minority could dwindle further. Let them all come. Mrs Calloway was a welcome recruit to the unseen crowds under the yew trees.

Fiona's brow was adorably puckered. Dan wanted to unpucker it, but it was no time for that sort of thing.

She said, 'I wish I could think of a new way of saying "We can't keep meeting like this".'

'Ben tiren,' said Dan, hoping the treacle in his voice would sweeten his personality. 'Mort o' treadlen.'

'*Treadling*,' said Fiona, suddenly laughing, but as though shocking herself by doing so. 'That's over the top.'

'Hereabouts, us ben usen they oldie words,' said Dan hopefully.

She pushed him away with her bicycle again. He had never before realised that a simple bicycle made such a good weapon of defence, or offence.

She still wanted him, or them, to do something positive to help Sandra Hedges. She was still cross with him because he said there was nothing they could, or should, do.

She said something about getting somebody called Francis Morley to help, since Dan was too lazy or too cowardly to do anything. Dan had heard of Francis Morley, from Lady Simpson. She made him sound like a mixture between James Bond and Sir Galahad. Very struck, young Francis had been, by Fiona Muspratt. The two of them got on like a house on fire the moment they met. They made a wonderful-looking couple, Lady Simpson said, *in this very room*, standing just where Dan was standing.

Francis was coming for another weekend pretty soon, said Lady Simpson, and it wasn't to see his boring old cousins.

With this formidable new contender in the field, it was more than ever necessary for Dan to do something positive. With a mixture of doggedness and frivolity, he set himself to make another plan.

Mildred Calloway in New York. It sounded like the title of an interminable novel by a pupil of Theodore Dreiser. (Dan, at the Grammar School, had been guided to Dreiser by the English teacher; he clearly remembered the smell of the unread volumes.) She was quite a lot younger than her husband. She had a grown-up son, married, but she had had him pretty young, and he was hardly thirty. That put her time in New York somewhere about 1954. Harry Curtis hardly a teenager then, and two thousand miles away.

Nothing like as good as the Sir George Simpson scenario. Something could still be made of it.

She was about twenty-two when she arrived in New York, working for the American office of a big, boring London company. Dan had heard quite a lot about this wonderful phase of Mildred Calloway's life, over the five years he had been doing odd jobs for them. (Very odd jobs, some of them had been.) Fiona, in five months, had heard a good deal more, owing to the more boastful and name-dropping terms on which she and Mildred met. Mildred Taylor-Smith, as she was then called (or as her parents decided the family was called), lived with a family in an apartment in the East Seventies. She spoke of it, even to Dan, with desperate nostalgia. Of course she loved Edwin and their house and life in Medwell Fratrorum, but, you know, or of course actually you don't, the *life* and *atmosphere* and *vitality* of New York . . . A girl of twenty-two, moderately pretty, with a quaint British accent, might have had quite a ball in New York in the middle fifties. Dan was quite unable to picture any of it. Black-and-white films about bootleggers, starring James Cagney, which he had seen in small cinemas when he worked at the bank in Milchester . . . no, that was long before. Sukie Bush Dan had known pretty well, and pretty well loved, but she was not born until 1963. The America of Ike and Dulles, post-Korea, pre-Vietnam, was it a swinging, permissive time? Wild parties, lots of mixed drinks, suspenders flashing when girls jived? Even somebody who finished up as Mildred Calloway might have started in all that.

Must have. The script required it. Dan wrote the script, sitting on the side of the road beside his bicycle, under hedge-row trees which were shedding their leaves like deaf-mutes undressing in slow motion, under flocks of long-tailed titmice which were hurrying through the branches, *peep-peep-peep*, on a collective errand of moderate urgency.

Mildred was an innocent slip of a thing from a country parsonage (or perhaps a suburban insurance brokerage).

Suddenly she was dropped, all dewy-fresh, into a garish and cynical world of bright light and deep shadow, hectic music, intoxication, tall men in white tuxedos, their hair touched with grey at the temples . . .

She had practically come out and said she had lived like that. 'Vitality.' What did that mean, in a big city, if it didn't mean speakeasies and . . . no no no – they'd disappeared more than twenty years earlier. Bars and nightclubs. Dan had never been to a nightclub in a big city, and he had difficulty imagining what people did there that was so wicked and so expensive. Whatever it was, Mildred had been led into doing it. *Dragged* into doing it, by some evil and masterful older woman. Like a painted mechanical doll, like a zombie, hopped to the gills on drink and drugs by her 'friends', she had danced with neckless and swarthy men at four o'clock in the morning, and then, and then, out on her feet, not knowing what she was doing, half-carried into somebody's apartment, the ultra-discreet Filipino houseboy, more drinks, the hidden cameras . . .

Photographs. Harry Curtis had come by photographs. Explicit and deeply compromising. The name of the subject, the date and place, written on the back. Research. Whatever became of Miss Mildred Taylor-Smith? Perhaps a stroke of luck – a news item about Mrs Mildred Calloway, née Taylor-Smith, of Woodbines, Medwell Fratrorum. That explained the time-lag.

Where were the photographs now? Obviously she took them when she murdered Harry Curtis. That, after all, was the point of the murder. They had been ashes, since midnight on the night of the murder, in the Calloways' incinerator. Dan was struck by the thought that he had himself, several times since that night, raked through those very ashes while tending the Calloways' incinerator . . . with part of his mind he was, by this time, pretty well believing the story. That was a good thing, if other people were going to believe it.

There was the whole other aspect to consider, as with Admiral Jenkyn, Sir George Simpson, Dan himself, and so forth. There was the matter of an alibi on the night of the murder. Dan knew the Calloways' house, inside and out. They had bought their cottage five years before, doubled it in size, renamed it Woodbines, created an absurdly lavish garden, put down mushroom wall-to-wall carpeting, retired, and been a local pest ever since. There were four bedrooms. Dan had slept, himself, in two of them: once in one of the single beds, with the Calloways' daughter-in-law Camilla, because the Calloways were there and it was the only place to hide, and the nicest place to hide; and once in the Calloways' own double bed, with somebody quite different, when he thought the Calloways were away . . . Yes, the old Calloways still shared a double bed, and it was unlikely that one of them could get up, and go downstairs, before midnight, dressed, and get the car out, and drive to the village, and commit a murder, and go home to bed again, without the other realising it. Ah, they were in it together, which was no more than the theories required which accused Admiral Jenkyn and Sir George Simpson.

Mr Calloway had done it, to protect his wife from persecution. No, the only person Edwin Calloway had ever protected was himself, and the only part of himself he protected was his bank balance. He loved being burgled, because he claimed insurance on things he had already sold. He was horrible, but he was not a credible murderer. Was she? Every woman was a credible murderer. Adorable Fiona said she would commit a murder, under certain extreme circumstances. Edwin would defend Mildred, after the event, to the extent of saying nothing. Any other course would gravely affect his social standing in the neighbourhood. With his wife in prison for life, there would be no more drinks for him at the Simpsons' . . .

Dan realised that he was once again falling into the trap of believing his fantasy. There were loose ends. How had Harry Curtis come by those dreadful, explicit, pornographic photographs? He had been given them by, or stolen them from, somebody who didn't know what they were worth. How had he, in turn, come by them? He had stolen them from the owner. He was a burglar, an ignorant young junkie who needed money or money's worth immediately. Just the sort of bloke Harry Curtis was always in contact with. Two thousand miles apart? The junkie was on the run. Why did the owner have the photographs? Why had he had them for maybe thirty years and never done anything about them? Why were they taken in the first place? Because that was how the man got his kicks. He was rich, with that fancy apartment (the apartment took surrealist, Busby Berkeley shape in Dan's mind) and that manservant (a silent fellow, who hissed and shook his own hands, unless that was a different sort of Oriental). He didn't need to blackmail people. He would never take that kind of risk. But the photographs gave him power over their subjects. Mildred had been in his power as long as she stayed in New York. That was why she had come home, and changed her name by getting married (there could be no other reason for marrying Edwin Calloway) and buried herself in the country. But she had not buried herself deep enough, which she realised when Harry Curtis spoke to her during the party in the Church Rooms.

Yes, of course he spoke to her. Why else would she murder him? He must have spoken to her. They were seen talking together, in a corner, earnestly. Of course she and Edwin would both deny that there had been such a conversation; or say that, if there had, it was conventional and meaningless and forgotten. That part of the script had already been written by Admiral Jenkyn and Sir George Simpson and Sandra Hedges.

Poor Mildred, driven to such lengths. It was a pity, on dramatic grounds, she did not look more like Joan Crawford.

Two mornings later, Dan was remaking a post-and-rail fence he had made for the Calloways four years earlier. The fence had built-in obsolescence. Making a fence was slow and careful work, the way Dan did it. Mrs Calloway brought him a cup of sweetened Indian tea, knowing that the peasantry did not like coffee or China tea. He tried to draw her out about New York, which she mentioned to him many times but only in general terms, since any detail would have taken him far out of his intellectual depth.

'I saw things that would amaze you,' she said, speaking slowly and loudly as she always did to Dan. 'Just as, I am sure, *you* have seen things that would amaze *me*.'

Dan put on a face that meant he wanted to be amazed.

She spoke not of nightclubs or obscene photographs, but of

the Met, the Frick Collection, Lord and Taylor, and a vacation at Easthampton on Long Island.

'Ben assiten,' said Dan, wondering if 'exciting', so pronounced, could be understood.

'Wildy exciting,' cried Mildred Calloway. 'A ferment!'

Dan's undisciplined mind pictured an enormous, bubbling vat of ready-mixed cocktail. She went indoors to answer the telephone. From the back she looked a little less improbable as the subject of an obscene photograph, but only a little. The word 'exciting' confirmed, for the obedient part of his mind, the literal truth of the whole story.

He would have felt compunction, but for the way Edwin robbed his insurance company and Mildred treated the girls in the post office.

He poured away the strong, sweet tea, and began hammering a four-inch nail into a fence-post. It was a job to be done with care, not something to hurry.

He left with his wages, but without any more about New York.

In the bar of the Chestnut Horse, at six o'clock, Dan contrived that somebody, other than himself, raised the topic of the Calloways; and then that somebody else, still not himself, mentioned Mrs Calloway's two years in New York.

'She tol' me, 'smornen, 'twere exciten,' said Dan, in the in-between voice he used in the Chestnut Horse.

The conversation threatened to be about New York, America generally, and recent developments on *Dallas*. Dan steered it back to Mrs Calloway's exciting life. As though falling from the lime trees in the churchyard opposite the pub, words drifted like wind-borne leaves into the conversation: 'wild', 'innocent'; 'taken advantage of'; 'cocktails', 'not used to the stuff'; 'older men'; and, at last, 'photographs'. The boat sailed pretty straight after that point was reached. He hardly had to touch the tiller.

By closing time there was a new murderer, a popular choice because unpopular. The motive was the strongest yet. The regulars mocked one another for having supposed that Sir

George Simpson did it. It was nice to have a woman murderer, too. It made a change, and it was fair. The regulars practised rigorous sexual discrimination in their lives, but not in their choice of murderers. Dan had inconspicuously left by the time this point was reached. He was trying to make it up to his mother for being so late with what she called her tea.

Jim Gundry heard about it at eleven o'clock in the morning, by which time the photographs had almost been seen and practically described. Jim Gundry had the sense, rare to a man so little given to self-examination, of reliving the recent past.

Edwin Calloway admitted to having spoken to the stranger, now known to have been Harry Curtis, at the party in the Church Rooms. He had admitted to this all along. He had come close to boasting about it. He had talked to the chap for a moment or two, since he was obviously lonely and knew nobody.

A moment or two!

It was just small-talk, chit-chat, the impact of the Service of Induction on an American Baptist.

Small-talk!

Probably nobody had overheard the conversation. There was a lot of noise in the Church Rooms, and what they were saying was not interesting enough to eavesdrop on.

Of course nobody overheard it, when he was off in a corner hearing about his wife being blackmailed!

Mildred Calloway repeated that she had not met or spoken to the stranger. It was unimportant whether this was true or not, believed or not; it changed nobody's thinking. Edwin had been the go-between.

The episode went to Dan's head a little. He got above himself. He wanted more and better suspects. That meant he needed more motives – the whole village could not be blackmail victims, and fairness demanded that suspects be mixed not only as to sex but also as to social class. Dan wanted more Snowy Burdens; he wanted Curly Godden and Harry Barnet and Ted Goldingham. He really wanted Jim Gundry, but even in his present mood of compassion-cum-euphoria he thought that would be a bit difficult.

He wondered about getting some real obscene photographs, and planting them about the place. But he had no idea how to come by such things; he had no idea what, specifically, they could be photographs of.

Certain people were automatically excluded from his list of candidates. His own mother, whose health would be imperilled by rage if she were arrested for murder. Dr Smith, who was necessary to his mother. Fiona Muspratt and her family, although in general Captain Muspratt might be an excellent choice. The Reverend Gordon Hedges, because his wife would be upset and she had enough on her mind. Vince Mellins and his wife, because they could not see well enough to stab anybody with a knife. Probably other names would strike him as inadmissible as he mentally went down the electoral roll of the neighbourhood.

Provided the notion of motive was treated imaginatively, there was no need for the murderer to have attended the Service of Induction, or the party in the Church Rooms. He simply had to know that Harry Curtis was stopping in one of the bedrooms over the Chestnut Horse. How would anybody know that? How would anybody not know that? The reservation had been made days before, and confirmed the day before. Ted Goldingham had not suddenly gone dumb. All his regulars would know the astonishing fact that an American, with another American, was coming out of season to stay at the pub. If it was known in the Chestnut Horse it was known in the post office, and if it was known in those places it was known all over the countryside. It was *better* if the murderer had not been to the Church Rooms. He had gone upstairs in the Chestnut Horse, during the party or during the service or during the afternoon. He lay in hiding, having found and nicked Harry Curtis's knife or having brought his own knife, and Harry Curtis walked into the trap.

Why? The current suspects, with the single exception of himself, were linked by the fact that they had all been to

America. It was no good pretending anybody else had been to America; anybody who'd been there would talk about it – probably, like Mildred Calloway, far too much. But Harry Curtis had been in London for a few days. There were people who'd been up to London during those days. Mr Potter of the Old Mill (not the one that was a fancy restaurant, the other and much nastier one near the village) – he'd been to London. He'd run into Harry Curtis in a Soho strip-club. They'd got talking, because the girls were too boring to talk to. Mr Potter had revealed that he came from a village called Medwell Fratrorum. It was Mr Potter who had brought Harry Curtis to the village and the Chestnut Horse, not anybody who had been anywhere near America . . . Dan knew, not intimately, the inside of the Potters' house. They shared a bedroom but not a bed. Mrs Potter must have known that Mr Potter went out and came back; probably she knew he did a murder in between. Why did he? The bar of the Chestnut Horse would supply the details, from its knowledge, and apathetic dislike, of Mr Potter. Mrs Potter was said to have been on the stage. She still wore purple lipstick. This would increase the probability of Mr Potter being the murderer.

Had any of the other nobs and near-nobs been to London while Harry Curtis was there? (None of the village would have been, so to call the other lot; it was impossible to imagine Curly Godden in London.) It was easy to find out. Dan bought some groceries at the post office on his way home for lunch. There were four gabby women in the shop, as well as the women who worked there. Into their conversation fell, like a pebble from heaven into a pool, the question: who went to London when Harry Curtis was there, and met him there, and caused him to come to Medwell, and murdered him the night of the Service of Redaction or summat? Answers would be supplied, in that place and by those and other persons, within twenty-four hours.

Dan's mother said that the groceries he had bought were the wrong sort, and too cheap or too expensive, and he was lowering himself by doing menial work, and she was not hungry.

A partial answer was supplied that same evening, in the Chestnut Horse. Dan did not have to cast any flies, or start any balls rolling. Discussion, and suspicion, were self-generating. Nobody talked about anything else.

Terence Barclay had been to London while Harry Curtis and Cora Smith were there. Terence Barclay had a twirly moustache and an eye for the girls. Everything instantly and beautifully fitted.

Up to something, off in London on his own, or why would he have gone all that way, him practically retired and all? That was where he met Cora Smith. It was her came to Medwell, to see her new friend, Harry Curtis coming along for company. Yes, it was that way, not the other way about. He gives his old woman the excuse he's going to church. He does go to church, so as to be seen there. Looks in at the party. Slips out, unnoticed. Nips round the corner to the side door of the pub, which Cora Smith has left on the latch for him. What he doesn't know is that Harry Curtis is there.

Obviously you murder a bloke in circumstances like that.

Dan knew that the Chestnut Horse was guessing quite right and quite wrong. Terence Barclay had not brought Cora Smith to Medwell, but he had met her there; he was experienced and on the look-out and he saw the come-hither in her eyes, which was there the moment she saw him. A few murmured words would fix time (at once), place (upstairs over the pub) and price (unguessable).

Possibly Harry Curtis had been aware of the arrangement and cheerful about it; possibly he was Cora Smith's pimp; possibly he had *made* the arrangement, and taken his cut. But it was not possible that Terence Barclay had murdered Harry Curtis. He left the pub long before Sandra Hedges' arrival; and she had gone secretly and stayed for twenty minutes.

Terence Barclay was a fine candidate from the perspective of the bar of the Chestnut Horse, but as things stood he was not a serious entry. He might become one. Dan put him in the pending tray.

Dan found it difficult to think while he bicycled home from the pub, because there were so many distractions, including the danger of death. If he tried to think he wobbled, and people drove much too fast. He was apt to wobble even if he didn't think, because he went so slowly, but thinking increased the peril, and seldom came up with anything.

This time it did. The idea was so screamingly obvious that it must have occurred to other people – it must have occurred to the police.

Ted Goldingham had done it.

It was true that the front stairs of the Chestnut Horse were visible to anyone standing behind the bar. It was almost certainly true that either Ted or Ivy Goldingham had been behind the bar throughout the evening, because they didn't trust their customers. (It would have been crazy, for example, to leave Curly Godden alone with a fruit-machine full of coins.) But Ted and Ivy were all the time – as it were alternately – popping through the door behind the bar to the kitchen behind or the cellar below. Picturing them, Dan thought of those nursery barometers with little wooden figures of a man and a woman that swung, one or the other, out into the open on a tiny wooden platform. The man meant rain. Ted had gone out of the back of the bar, through the larder to the passage, along that to the foot of the stairs, up the stairs to nick what he could out of Harry Curtis's luggage. Ivy had seen him on the stairs, but nobody else had because they were all facing the other way. You did, at a bar. You didn't look over your shoulder. If you did a thing as stupid as that at the Chestnut Horse, somebody would drink your drink.

Yes, Ted Goldingham ran upstairs and into the American's room. He wouldn't worry about fingerprints – it was his house, and his fingerprints were naturally on everything. He found some books, papers, documents. He put them in his pocket in the hope that there was something incriminating in them – something that would enable him to blackmail Harry Curtis. The biter bit. Very nice irony. All clear so far. It must have happened like that, or why were there no papers of any sort found in the room? Then he found the commando dagger, hidden among Harry Curtis's spare pyjamas. At that point Harry Curtis came back and found him.

Anybody would stab a bloke, found in such circumstances, especially if he happened to have a dagger ready in his hand.

Stabbed him in the back. Would Harry Curtis turn his back on a thief, at a moment like that? Yes, something distracted him, made him turn round for a moment, something Ted tossed across the room, a noise from the bar, Ivy Goldingham's laugh . . .

The dead man's pockets had been full of money. Well, obviously, Ted Goldingham panicked. He was squeamish. It was one thing to lash out, almost instinctively, to save himself from going to prison; it was another to go through the pockets of a corpse.

Probably there was all sorts of incriminating stuff in the papers Ted had pinched. But it turned out not to be any use to him. You couldn't blackmail a dead man. So it had all gone into the incinerator behind the pub.

It would be extremely hard to prove that Ted Goldingham *had* done it; but Dan did not see how Ted could prove that he *hadn't*. That was rather the case with all the other 'suspects'.

Of course it might have been Ivy Goldingham, or Debbie Chandler. By all accounts, Debbie had put on a wonderful act, screaming when she 'discovered' the body.

The problem about believing all this was Harry Curtis turning his back. It was not a problem anybody would have who had heard Ivy Goldingham's laugh. In one important respect the new version was *easier* to believe than any of the others, because it solved the riddle of the pub's side door having been locked.

Pretty watertight, but the Chestnut Horse was not the place to launch it. The Simpsons' was the place, and Lady Simpson was the audience. She was an excellent audience, because she had hated suspecting any of her neighbours (she did not count the Goldinghams as neighbours) and she quite disliked suspecting her husband.

Dan said he had heard the story as fact.

'From *whom*, Dan?'

'A-b'lieves 'twere Massr Hadge,' said Dan, blinking bashfully and twisting his cap in his hands so that he appeared to be strangling a squirrel.

'Mr Hadge? Hodge? Hedges? Surely not Mr Hedges?'

' 'Twere *ol'* Massr Hadge,' said Dan, as though authenticating the story.

The Potters were giving a drinks party that evening, which Dan knew about because Fiona was going with her parents. All the suspects together, except himself and Ted Goldingham. Confusedly, Dan supposed they would drink Bloody Marys or Sangria. The Simpsons were certainly going, and the story would gain immediate currency. There was no knowing who 'old Mr Hadge' would be identified as.

Francis Morley was at the Potters' party, coming with the Simpsons. He was wearing a beautiful dark grey suit and a regimental tie. His face lit up when he saw Fiona coming in behind her parents. It really did. Lady Simpson said so afterwards. He had been abstracted, in spite of his beautiful manners, glancing constantly towards the door, waiting for someone. It was not difficult to guess who he was waiting for, the one beautiful girl expected at the party (except for dear little Mrs Hedges and that dear little Cora Smith, who drank nothing). When Fiona came in it was as though somebody had thrown a switch behind Francis's eyes. He grinned and twinkled and *charged* across the room. She looked equally pleased to see him. She was heard thanking him for some flowers. They seemed to be alone together in the middle of the party.

Young love was therefore one of the topics of the evening. The other was the fact of Ted Goldingham having murdered Harry Curtis.

9

Ted Goldingham was a flash in the pan, a fringe candidate, a joke. Dan had to go after bigger game. His motives, in devising the next episode, were more mixed than anybody's motives had any business to be.

First there was Sandra Hedges.

Dan had an excellent memory; he was not apt to forget anything that forcibly struck him. He knew that as long as he was sane, and probably long after he was insane, he would remember the look of frozen misery, blinking on-off like a flashlight in a horror film, in the middle of that cheerful and baffling Service of Induction. And her coming away from the Chestnut Horse, in the dark in the middle of the night, with no expression at all.

Second there was Fiona.

Dan was flummoxed. She liked him. He made her laugh. That was the crux and the irony, the good news and the bad. If he had not made her laugh, right then at the beginning, outside the post office, they would never have had any relationship at all, never have been the friends they were. Bully for laughter. But laughing at him set an exact limit on their relationship; it was a chain-link fence. The fence allowed him a certain latitude, like a pony in a paddock: but if there was a gate Dan could not find it. He wanted Fiona's respect. Admiration. Awe. He wanted to be the person Fiona gaped at, awestruck, not the person she laughed at.

The person she gaped at was Francis Morley. Dan had not actually met this person, but he had had a good look at him, and he had listened to him chatting to people in the post office. He topped Dan by inches, he was younger, he was richer, he was a gentleman. This was all bad, but the worst of it was that he was a good bloke. People liked him, and they were right. Fiona liked him, and she was right. There was a kind of inevitability about them coming together. Dan chose to defy the inevitable. At least, he reckoned to try.

A third factor was Jim Gundry.

The gloomy policeman had constituted himself, years before, leader of the anti-Dan club. There were plenty of other candidates for the leadership, but Jim hung on to it. It was harassment. Dan was an oppressed minority. If he had been an ethnic group, there would have been articles in the *Guardian* about him.

Jim Gundry was doing absolutely nothing about finding the murderer of Harry Curtis. He was failing in his duty as a public servant. He was sheltering, cravenly, behind the fact that a senior officer had taken charge of the investigation. It was hardly surprising that he was shirking his duty of finding the murderer, since he was himself the murderer.

It was shocking that a man should so far betray the trust reposed in him by the public, by Her Majesty the Queen. Something had better be done about it, by some caring person who put public duty before self.

Fiona might still laugh at him, but there would be new respect in her laughter. Sandra Hedges might still be headed for unthinkable calamity, but he would be buying her a bit more time.

Opportunity? Motive?

Jim Gundry had exactly the same opportunity as anybody else. He only had his wife with him, in that hovel they called the Police Station, their daughter Julie being off in a far place teaching. (Dan wondered if she were teaching the little girls some of the things he knew she knew.) As far as that went, Jim Gundry was placed like most of the other suspects. No, no – Dan was being silly – Jim had far more opportunity than any other suspect, because he had a key to the side door of the Chestnut Horse. Ted Goldingham didn't know about that. Jim had had a copy made of the key they found on the body, before it was locked away in Milchester. Or Ted Goldingham's predecessor had given Jim Gundry's predecessor a key, so he could keep an eye on the place when it was empty. Some of the nobs did that – gave Jim Gundry a key to the house for when they were away. Dan would rather have given his eye-teeth to a hungry terrier, but it was a thing a publican might do. Jim Gundry's possession of that key had first to be brought about and then discovered. Simple, practical stuff, more in Dan's line than all this thinking.

Motive? Had Harry Curtis been making lewd advances at Beryl Gundry? Did Jim Gundry fancy that Mrs Cora Smith, who seemed now to be a fixture in the village, although she would have been long gone with Harry Curtis alive? Beryl must once have looked a bit like Cora Smith, difficult as that now was to believe, or how could you account for her daughter Julie? But it took a bit of swallowing, that one. Dan would have been happy to swallow it, but he doubted if anyone else would.

Dan wanted to consult Fiona. He had great respect for her intelligence, and she knew the ways of bluebottles, her father having been one. But to consult her was hardly the way to gain her awestruck respect, and that remained a priority.

Harry Curtis could have had nothing on Jim Gundry. For one thing, he had only been in the village for about seven hours before he was killed; and for another, nobody had anything on Jim Gundry – there was nothing on him to have, not until he started killing people.

There wasn't anything in Jim Gundry's past. He'd always been a right Puritan – he must have been, to have married Beryl. There wasn't anything in Beryl's past, either, for the same reason in reverse.

Harry Curtis must have had something Jim Gundry wanted so badly that he killed to get it. The secret of eternal youth? Documents that enabled him to blackmail Sir George Simpson? Mrs Cora Smith? A design for a death-ray, the philosopher's stone, a collection of dirty postcards? (How they did keep cropping up!)

Dan was almost in a mood to telephone Fiona, at her office, from the post office. Without her advice he was stuck. It had never happened to him before.

It came to him, at this moment of humiliation, that a lot of the girls he had known would make more sense of all this than he was making. Suki Bush from Florida. Natasha Chapman, the little actress from Surbiton. Juanita Jones, black, student of English literature, cleverest of the lot. Julie Gundry . . .

Julie. Dan was staggered that the penny had taken so long to drop. He had mentioned Julie to himself, thinking how strange it was that a couple like Jim and Beryl could produce such a toothsome daughter, thinking of her with affection and gratitude . . . He had been dangling Julie, as it were, before his own eyes, and only now did it strike him that she was the answer.

Julie, not long qualified, was teaching at a school near Guildford. That was near London. Dan had never been to Guildford, but he pictured it in terms of the Potters, the Calloways and the Simpsons. Somebody who lived there would go to London for laughs. Julie liked laughs, all right. So she went to London while Harry Curtis was there. He was a predator, a flashy villain, a sort of Mack the Knife. She was an innocent Wessex girl, landed all alone in a dormitory town . . . No, she wasn't so very innocent, and she obviously wasn't all alone, not a girl as pretty as that, but still she was putty in the hands of an operator like Harry Curtis.

Julie told Harry Curtis about Medwell Fratrorum, there in the Soho nightclub he'd lured her to – told him about her Dad the village policeman and a lot else besides. That was why he came. *What* was why he came? Nobody would ever know, probably, exactly why he came, but he came because of what Julie had said to him.

What he didn't know was that Julie also told her father about Harry Curtis. Yes, she told him on the telephone, maybe early in the evening, the night of the Service of Induction. Either 'I want you to be nice to a friend of mine who's coming to Medwell', or 'Look out for a horrible villain who's coming to Medwell.' Maybe she said 'friend' and he understood 'villain'. Jim would be like that, ever so protective, much good that had done Julie. Of course Julie would deny such a telephone call, and so would Jim, and Julie would deny having been to London, and Beryl would back them both up . . .

But somebody had seen Julie in London. Terence Barclay, of course. Wilfred Potter, too. They'd both been to the big city at the operative time. It was practically established that they'd both been up to no good in Soho strip-clubs, that they'd both fallen foul of Harry Curtis. Well, they'd both seen Julie Gundry with Harry Curtis, in the same club or different clubs. They'd both said so in confidence to somebody, though of course they'd deny it in public.

They said it not of themselves but of each other. Terence Barclay said, 'When Wilfred Potter was in London he went to a Soho strip-club, naughty old thing, and who do you think he saw? Better not tell Jim Gundry about the way his daughter's been carrying on.' And Wilfred Potter said, 'Who would have thought it of old Terence? Just his luck that he ran into somebody from Medwell.'

As soon as those two stories got about, they wouldn't be speaking to one another. The viper's tongue, the treacherous friend, insinuation, slander . . . Dan thought it would be nice for them both, not to have to speak to the other, but he hoped the upshot wouldn't be trouble for Julie.

The whole scheme was chancy, overly-complicated, and unacceptably manipulative. Dan was extravagantly proud of it. He faced with something like relish putting it into immediate operation.

It was common knowledge that there were four keys to the side door of the Chestnut Horse. The other, the fifth, the one in Jim Gundry's possession, had still to be conjured into existence. One on a hook on a board on the wall behind the bar of the Chestnut Horse, where a fruitfly could not have got at it unobserved. One on Ted Goldingham's key-ring, which he kept on the end of a chain in a pocket of whatever he was wearing. One in the possession of the deceased at the time of his death, assumed now to be in a safe in the Milchester Police Station. One in the possession, on that night, of Mrs Cora Smith. What had become of that one? Probably she had given it to Ted Goldingham, or she had given it to the police and they had given it to Ted Goldingham. It was conceivable that she still had it. If Ted had it, where was it?

It was easy to find out, by sliding the topic of keys into the conversation in the bar in the evening.

'Never you mind about my ruddy keys, Dan ruddy Mallett,'

said Ted Goldingham. 'I'll start worryin' about them when you got one.'

Dan thought that this, as a comment on his personality, was lacking in delicacy. But the ball, once started, gained momentum, because apart from the local murder there was very little for those men, who saw one another daily, to find to talk about.

Sid Jolly, who sometimes played the harmonium in the Baptist Chapel in Milchester, turned away from the fruit-machine and picked up a fag-end. Hearing the word 'key', he began to tell a story about transposing something into B Flat. Nobody listened to Sid. As a Baptist he had no business in the pub. The conversation proceeded, heedless of Sid Jolly's contribution. Vince Mellins came in, heard Sid talking about 'flats', and deduced that he was talking about the Monk's House, outside the village, which had been turned into three flats. It was more difficult to ignore Vince than Sid, but to the Chestnut Horse regulars it was possible.

Meanwhile it was becoming evident that Ted Goldingham had a grievance. He nearly always had a grievance: Dan thought that Ted without a grievance would be like a peewit without a crest – all wrong, somehow. Sometimes Ted's grievances went on for days, like his socks; sometimes there was a fresh one daily, like Ivy Goldingham's aprons. The truculence of Ted's manner to Sid Jolly, and to Dan, suggested a grievance not new but dormant, like an artichoke plant in the winter, brought back to life by something one of them said.

It related to keys, as Dan had hoped. It related to the keys of the side door of the pub.

There one of them was where it belonged, right and tight on its peg on the board above the bar; it had a little buff-coloured tag, like a luggage-label, so Ted knew which was which. Here another one was where it belonged, on a ring on a chain in Ted's hip pocket. This had no tag. Ted only had two other Yale locks, and he knew which key was which. All the other doors – cellar, garage and so forth – had mortice locks; the keys, comparatively massive, lived on a shelf below the bar. A third key had been among the effects of the murdered man; the police still had it. Ted Goldingham had a minor grievance about that, but only a minor one.

The fourth key, ah. That was what made Ted's brow darken. The police still had that one, too, and it was ruddy inconvenient. Why was it inconvenient, when nobody was staying in the bedrooms, and the Goldinghams and Debbie could get to the bedrooms by the front stairs? It just was. The police were being unreasonable and inconsiderate. Talking to Jim Gundry was like talking to a brick wall. He said the key was in the safe in Milchester and there was nothing he could do about it. Ted wanted evidence that he'd even tried to do anything about it.

Ted reacted negatively to the suggestion that he could get more keys cut. Why should he be at that expense and trouble? All he wanted was his rights and his property, and the police were riding rough-shod.

The population of the bar, a dozen strong, mumbled agreement, because it made life easier to agree with Ted Goldingham. It was not certain if Vince Mellins knew what he was agreeing with. There was no surge of warm fellow-feeling, of sympathetic indignation. Nobody cared very much about Ted's keys, except Dan, who hid his interest, and virtually hid himself behind his pint of beer.

Only two keys in circulation, if you could call being on a peg behind the bar being in circulation. The problem was numerically simpler but in other ways more difficult.

Ted kept the three keys of his car on that ring in his pocket – door, ignition and petrol filler-cap. Dan did not know what the other two Yale locks were. He did not know why some modern cars had three keys. He had never burgled the Chestnut Horse, not to say properly burgled, and he had never borrowed Ted Goldingham's car. Ted was the sort of man who locked his car and then locked his garage, and his own bedroom window looked out over the garage. But the car was the way in, so to speak.

Dan got some Yale keys, which looked like any other Yale keys. He found them here and there. He did not know what they opened. Probably they opened nothing – they were simply old keys of locks that had long been broken or changed. He was not robbing anybody of anything of value – at least, he did not think Lady Simpson or Mrs Calloway would be inconvenienced.

He borrowed a nearly full five-litre can of sage-green emulsion paint. He could have borrowed enamel paint, more expensive and stronger smelling, but the emulsion would come off in soap and water, so it was more considerate to use it. Dan felt a conscious glow of good-neighbourliness, taking the trouble to make sure it was emulsion paint he borrowed. It was more than the Potters needed, for repainting their spare room, and it was the wrong colour anyway for a north-facing room. Objectively considered, it was a favour he was doing them.

Most of what the Goldinghams needed was delivered, by the brewers and the wholesalers and so forth. For their own food they shopped mostly in the post office. But Ted went to Milchester once a week, to bank his takings and because there was no good fishmonger nearer. Ivy almost always went with him. They locked the place up, but there was always somebody about keeping an eye on it. They always left pretty sharp at half past nine, because it was easier to find a place to park and easier to do the shopping, even though they had to wait for the bank to open. If they were not back by opening time, Debbie opened up for them. There was no trade to speak of, first thing. It was not odd that Dan knew all this; it would have been odd if he had not.

Dan got up very early in the morning, before the sky was light, before the bantams or the doves were awake. Probably his mother was awake. He hoped to be back in time to give her a late breakfast. She would be angry at her breakfast being late, even though, when it came to the point, she would eat very little of it. With a lifetime of his father and himself, she ought to have got used by now to irregular meal-times; but she never would. It was one of the things that set her brooding, and it was bad for her arthritis.

Dan tried to get away without disturbing the dogs, but it was no more possible to deceive them than it was to deceive his mother. Pansy, the cross old pointer, pretended not to be excited to see him. There was much in common between Pansy and Dan's mother, except that Pansy had a very good appetite.

It was perfectly still. There was a hint of ground-frost. Everything would be wet when the sun struck, but now grass and weeds slightly crunched, drily, like wrapping paper. Dan wobbled away on his bicycle as the sky was just beginning to pale.

He was wearing corduroy trousers (not the comic-peasant ones), a heavy dark sweater, a tweed cap, woollen gloves, and boots with rubber soles. He had enough clothes to be warm, but not enough to hamper his movements. In his pocket were half a dozen unidentified Yale keys. Over the handlebars of the bicycle was slung, by its own carrying-handle, the can of four and a half litres of sage-green emulsion paint.

Dan thought he would see nobody. He did not want to be seen. He was doing nothing illegal, yet – nothing, for him, even so very suspicious – but the can of paint would take a bit of explaining. Nobody went off decorating before dawn.

Dan took a long way round, so that he approached the village from the far end. His way took him past the Jenkyns' riverside house, dark and silent, almost invisible from the road in near-darkness and the mist from the river. Was Admiral Jenkyn tossing with worry, at being a murder suspect? Mrs Jenkyn, at the threat of a charge of being an accessory? The Reverend Gordon Hedges, at the occasional, fleetingly visible misery on his wife's face? Mrs Sandra Hedges, at what she had done, and why she had done it, and the imminence of her child, and the stammer of the telephone, and the heavy knock on the door . . .

It was worth while, what he was doing. It would have been worth while even if he was killing only one bird with his stone, but his plan was to kill three.

Dan bicycled slowly, alert for any sign of life, past the cricket pitch on the edge of the village. He could just see the church tower, darker on dark, over its petticoats of yews and lime trees. In the rough grass at the edge of the cricket pitch there was a strange new pyramid, fifteen foot high, faggots and brushwood. The bonfire, for Guy Fawkes Day three days later. The Boys'

Club had been building it, under the direction of Admiral Jenkyn and the Reverend Gordon Hedges. Would Mrs Hedges venture out, in the cold and dark and damp, for bonfire and fireworks and gluhwein? Yes, of course she would, if she hadn't been arrested by then.

Dan would be there. He had a childish love of fireworks. He went 'Ooh' when the rockets went up, and 'Aah' when they exploded and came down, in unison with the village children. He would not drink any gluhwein, though – the wine the Admiral put in fell far short of his standards.

Cottages. Nobody going to work yet. Nobody hereabouts worked night shifts in hospitals or factories. Dan's bicycle tyres whispered on the frosty tarmac, and the chain clicked like a tired clock. There was no sound of bird or beast, man or machine.

Dan stopped and dismounted by the wall of the churchyard. He unshipped the paint-can from his handlebars. It would be easier bicycling back, without the swinging weight of the paint. He swung the bicycle over the wall, and propped it out of sight in the churchyard.

He had always felt friendly vibrations, from ten centuries of the village's dead. He did so now. They were helping him, as best they could, by providing refuge for his bicycle.

He picked up the paint, and prowled towards the Chestnut Horse.

If anyone saw him now, anywhere near the Chestnut Horse with that can of paint, the mission was aborted. He would walk on by, and probably take the paint back to the Potters. He had no personal use for such a quantity of paint, and he had no use for so much as a teaspoonful of paint of that colour. He would appear at the Old Mill – that Old Mill – as early as he reasonably could, make noises like a Wessex pixie, be understood in the end to say that he had found the paint-can in the village and known it to be theirs, and hope they didn't notice that he was wearing more or less conventional clothes. That would all be a terrible pity, and his mother's breakfast late to no purpose.

Also he would have to think of another plan, which was a rotten way of spending his time, to be compared adversely with (for example) being kissed on the nose by Fiona.

Dan crept safely past the Mellins's cottage, and into the alleyway beside the pub. He passed the locked side door, and emerged into the yard behind the building. This was the bit the Goldinghams' window overlooked. It was a good deal darker here than in the broad road between the pub and the church. It was liable to be booby-trapped with empty beer-crates and abandoned bicycles, left by blokes who didn't trust themselves to get home on two wheels. At the back of the yard, its door facing the back of the pub, was the outbuilding which was now the garage. Next to it was a higher and more massive outbuilding, once some kind of barn, now the Gents'. Dan wondered fleetingly what people had done when the barn was still a barn. Between the Gents' and the garage ran another narrow, cobbled passage. Dan slipped along it, past the open door of the Gents'. There was a powerful reek of disinfectant. You could say what you liked about Ted Goldingham, but he did use plenty of chemical. With clients like Curly Godden it wasn't a thing you'd stint.

The passage debouched on to the pub's garden. There was nearly half an acre, used for nothing much. It was not a place in which you could imagine painted furniture, gay umbrellas, long cool drinks. The only gardens like that were private: the nearest Dan got to enjoying them was painting the furniture. Ted Goldingham grew a few vegetables; otherwise he got a man with a power scythe to come two or three times a summer to keep the place tidy. Ted didn't have time to do the garden and he didn't have time to enjoy the garden, so except for a few rows of sprouts and broccoli there wasn't any garden.

It looked better in the dark. As a place to wait it was better than the roof of the garage, and much, much safer. It was highly unlikely that anybody would come into the garden before the Goldinghams set off for Milchester. If anybody did, Dan and his paint were pretty well hidden in the scrubby bushes behind the garage.

There was a way out at the bottom of the garden, through another garden and on to the cricket pitch. The garden belonged to Enid and Bob Cranston (they were always put that way round) who would welcome Dan as a trespasser as much as a herd of cows, or a plague of rabbits, or a bus-load of schoolchildren. All the same, it gave Dan an option, and he wanted a few of them.

Sitting waiting in a secret place was something Dan had spent a lot of his life doing, ever since he left the bank, where he spent a lot of time sitting waiting in a public place. It was a part of his profession. Woodcock did not fly into your net, or pheasant walk into your angles, if you ran about after them. He had learned a kind of suspended animation, not asleep – very far from asleep – but not making any demands on himself. It was a rest. He had no need to think – he had done all his thinking, with the result that he was here in the garden of the Chestnut Horse, at seven o'clock in the morning, with nearly five litres of evil-coloured emulsion paint. Further serious thinking would only confuse him, and might even make him change his mind about the day's project. He fell to day-dreaming instead, all of him torpid except his eyes and ears, which remained hypersensitive alarms connected to bells in his head.

His day-dreams concerned Fiona. They moved into areas of the wildest fantasy. He had plenty of time for them.

A little before eight, according to his mental clock, he heard noises from the upstairs of the pub, and shortly afterwards from downstairs. He heard a door open: Ivy Goldingham getting in the milk from the doorstep. Muted clangs: Ivy putting on the kettle and beginning to fry the eggs. A kind of bellow: Ted Goldingham trying to find his socks. Household noises – the same sort of thing was going on all over the village.

Dan thought of fried eggs, and he almost cried. Then he thought about the sort of tea Ivy Goldingham would make, and he felt better about not sharing their breakfast.

More clangs. Voices. The throb of water in elderly plumbing. Ted getting the bar takings out of his safe. They were both downstairs, and Ted would probably stay there. But Ivy would go upstairs again before they went off to Milchester. Women always did. Dan wanted to get on the roof of the garage, but not while Ivy was where she could see it.

Dan rose to his feet, growing upwards rather than suddenly standing. By climbing on to a water-butt, he could get his chin on the roof. The roof sloped upwards at about twenty degrees, in a single plane, from his chin to the front of the garage. It was covered in a kind of rubberised felt, greenish, in colour not unlike the Potters' emulsion paint. From above, Dan would be as visible on it as a dead crow on a bed-sheet (perhaps not the Goldinghams' bed-sheet). From where he was, he could see the upper halves of the upstairs windows of the pub – the two windows of the bedroom, and the one of the landing outside it. The other bedrooms – the hotel, so to say – were away to the right and faced over Vince Mellins's. Dan stood like a stick, listening. Kitchen clangs. Ivy still downstairs. The washing-up would be left for Debbie. Ted would be reading the paper at the kitchen table, getting in Ivy's way as she cleared away break-fast. That also was probably happening all over the village.

Silence. Dan imagined footsteps, Ivy clumping upstairs. He convinced himself he could hear the rustle as Ted turned the pages of the *Mirror*, though he knew this was impossible. It was full daylight by now, the clocks having gone back to Greenwich Mean Time. The back of the pub faced west, so that the rising sun threw the interior of the Goldinghams' bedroom into deep shadow. It threw the roof of the garage into a kind of shadow, too, but not nearly such a deep one.

Dan thought he saw a flicker of movement behind one of the bedroom windows – Ivy upstairs, putting on the lipstick she only wore for Milchester. Soon Ted's feet would crunch across the yard to the garage.

Dan climbed down from the water-butt, and put the paint on it. The can was very white although the paint was green. Ted Goldingham's car was white, just as white: Ted kept a very clean car.

Dan heard Ted's approaching footsteps. What he had to listen for was the crash of the door when Ivy shut it behind her, that or some clear indication that she was downstairs. What he heard was the click of the key going into the garage door, the clunk as the key turned, the scream as Ted lifted the metal roll-over door, then a sort of shuffle as Ted eased along the narrow gap between the car and the wall of the garage.

The moment Ted started the car would be a good time for getting on to the roof, but only if Ivy was downstairs. With the noise Ted was making, Dan could hear nothing from the pub, and with the glare of the sun and the pub silhouetted against it he could see nothing behind the glass of the windows. He became suddenly certain that he was wasting his time, that the whole scheme was ridiculous and doomed to failure.

Dan heard the small sound of Ted unlocking the car door, and the larger sound of his groan as he fitted himself into the driving seat. He would warm up the engine for a moment before he started backing out of the garage. (Dan assumed he would back out – it was much easier backing out than backing in.)

Nothing could be heard of Ivy's movements over the noise of Ted's self-starter, then the noise of his engine. Ted tooted his horn as he warmed up the engine. (It was one of the ways you could tell about a marriage, Dan thought – watch out for the future if the husband toots his horn to hurry his wife out of the house; but the Goldinghams had stuck with one another for thirty years, and would probably go on doing so.)

There was a scream from the house, from downstairs – Ivy saying that she was coming, telling him to stop making that bloody awful noise with the horn. Dan thought he heard Ted's macho grunt of impatience.

Ivy would wait for Ted to back out before she tried to get into the car. She was not built for sidling along between the car and the wall.

Dan heaved the big paint-can on to the roof of the garage. He followed it, no part of himself more than half the height of the can. Lifting the can along, while remaining flat, was awkward, but it could not be pushed because of the noise on that abrasive roofing-felt. He himself, wriggling, was making an uncomfortable amount of noise, but he thought the engine would be drowning it.

It was possible that Ivy would go upstairs once more, for something forgotten, for a purse or a scarf or gloves. If she did, she would sure enough look out of the bedroom window to see where Ted had got to with the car. She would sure enough see Dan. She would squawk loud enough for Ted to hear, over the noise of the car. Dan would remove himself, risking the passage of the Cranstons' garden, relying thereafter on blank denial. That was just how it would probably be, and Dan risked making a gigantic fool of himself.

He had no idea where Ivy was. She might have locked the

door and crossed the yard. She might now be standing by the garage. There was no particular reason, if so, that she should look up at the edge of the roof; there was no particular reason she shouldn't.

It had to be risked, for all the reasons that had put him in this ridiculous position. He crawled forward, and peeped over the front edge of the roof. Ivy was there. She was looking crossly into the garage. Ted, having been kept waiting, was getting his own back by keeping her waiting. Dan was surprised that no exhaust was visible from the back of the car as it warmed up in the garage.

The note of the engine changed, as Ted got into reverse. Dan lifted the paint-can to the edge of the roof; he kept himself so low that Ivy, if she looked up, would think a can of paint had arrived during the night, by magic, on the roof.

The car came forwards out of the garage. Ted had backed in. The car was rear-engined, so that noise was coming from the back which Dan had thought was the front. Ted stopped with the back of the car four feet from the garage. Ivy advanced. Now or never.

Dan poured the whole can of paint on to the rear window of the car.

10

It was unfortunate, really, that so much of the paint went over
Ivy Goldingham. It was not something Dan had intended. She
had darted forward to shut the garage door. Obviously that was
their routine – Ted drove the car out of the garage, and Ivy shut
the door before she climbed in. Probably it was a thing that
happened almost everywhere. Dan was a bit appalled, and even
contrite, at having turned Ivy into a pillar of sage-green emulsion. But there was plenty of paint on the car – the rear window
was almost totally obscured.

Ivy ran screaming back towards the house, to get the paint off
herself. Dan thought, with unusual compunction, about sage-
green dollops all over the Chestnut Horse. He did not linger,
either to watch Ivy or to feel guilty. It would be more than ever a
waste, if the thing did not come to a successful conclusion. Dan
slid backwards down the slope of the roof, taking the empty
paint-can. He threw the can as far as he could into the middle of
the garden. It would be found, but not immediately. Meanwhile the paint would seem to have arrived from the sky by
magic.

Ted, at the wheel of the car, could have seen nothing above
and behind the car. Now he could see nothing behind the car.
By the time he was out of the car, making dangerous noises, the
paint-can was in the scrub and Dan was on his feet by the
water-butt.

Ivy would be fully occupied for as long as Dan needed. With
any luck Ted would too. Dan slipped along the passage between
the garage and the Gents', and sneaked a look round the corner.
Ted was out of the car and behind it, and staring at the paint
with an expression that would have been comic if it had not
contained so large an element of tragedy. He had got out of the
car on the right-hand side, the driver's side, so that he was

half-facing Dan. Dan wished the scene was being played in America, where Ted would have been on the other side, and would now have his back to Dan.

Would Ted realise it was emulsion paint – that he could get most of it off with a hosepipe? Was there a stand-pipe in the garage or anywhere in the yard? The answer seemed to be no to one or both questions, because Ted followed Ivy into the house, more nearly running than anybody had ever seen him.

Dan went like a mouse to the side of the car. He opened the passenger's door, nearer to him, the minimum amount. He was still wearing gloves. He wriggled in, and reached across under the steering wheel. He took the key out of the dash, and with it the other keys on the ring. He got out of the car. Using what cover there was, he scampered to the side door. He tried the three Yale keys on the ring in the lock of the door. One wouldn't go in. The second went in but wouldn't turn. The third, as might have been expected, was the one. Dan thought he was not visible from anywhere where there would be anyone watching. There were bellowings from inside the pub, but they were the bellows of somebody bothered about paint, not those of somebody seeing Dan Mallett trying keys in a side door.

Dan took the key off the ring, and put it by itself in an inside pocket. He put another key on the ring in its place, a key that looked roughly the same but probably opened nothing.

It was to be hoped that Ted Goldingham did not have occasion to unlock the side door for the next few hours.

Dan tossed the bunch of keys into the middle of the yard. Ted would find them quick enough; he would have to assume that he had taken the ignition out of the dashboard, and dropped the bunch on his way to the house, distracted by the miraculous draught of paint.

Nine-forty. The men who worked had gone to work. A few women were already plodding towards the post office, and two girls were waiting at the bus stop. A semi-retired insurance broker, on his way to a 'business' lunch, went up the village street in a Volvo. Dan would have liked either a much larger crowd or a much smaller one, but this was the crowd he had. He emerged from the alleyway and started towards the river, trying to combine invisibility with an air of careless unconcern.

Nobody in the outside world yet knew of the outrage in the back yard of the Chestnut Horse; nobody would therefore pay particular attention to one small bad character coming out of that yard; so nobody would remember that he was there. Dan examined the logic of this, as he made himself stroll back towards his bicycle, and found it faulty. He had relied, in a woolly way, on the intervention of a couple of lorries, or of somebody delivering frozen peas to the post office, or of Vince Mellins having a fit, to distract attention from himself. Things like that usually happened, but nothing like that happened. He tried to resemble a mouse, but he felt like a mouse in a spotlight.

He was invisible when he recovered his bicycle, but he was visible when he mounted it and rode away.

His mother's breakfast was not so very late, but she said it was.

Dan could have bicycled to Milchester, but he felt disinclined to do so. As a matter of policy he seldom borrowed vehicles by day, but he borrowed Fred Dawson's van that day. One of the merits of Fred's van was that Dan could get to it, and get away in it, unseen by anybody except Fred's hens; another was that Dan had a key to it. He had borrowed Fred's van quite often, for errands involving cargoes or journeys of more than ten miles, but usually in the middle of the night. He could not afford to wait until the middle of the night, and the service he required in Milchester was only available by day. Because Fred was a blacksmith, his van was well known among the nobs and farmers who owned ponies. This was, if anything, an advantage – nobody would have the gall to take a well-known van, in the middle of the morning, into the middle of Milchester, without the knowledge and consent of the owner.

Fred was in his forge. Fred's wife was attending to the music on the mid-morning, pictureless television. Dan drove the van away, with the key he had acquired the same day Fred acquired the van. He had never held a licence or taken a test, but his driving was skilful and confident – erring, perhaps, on the side of over-confidence. He was dressed in the clothes for pouring paint on a publican's car, which were the same as the clothes for having spare keys cut in the ironmonger's shop in the Butter-market in Milchester. He thought neither he nor the van would be noticed in the bustle of Milchester.

He was wrong. Fiona Muspratt saw him. The estate agency she worked for had offices in the Buttermarket, a few doors from the ironmonger. He saw her seeing him. For the first time since they had met, and unimaginably, he did not want to talk to her. He ducked into a supermarket, and peered between the posters glued to its window. Luckily she was in a hurry, going somewhere on foot with a box-file under her arm. She stared hard at the supermarket, seemed to be about to cross the street to follow him into it, but turned and went on her way. Dan bought some frozen cod fillets, as an excuse for sheltering in the supermarket, and dropped them into a litter-bin on his way out. They would have been perfectly all right, but his mother wouldn't touch frozen fish. 'Gi's ye the cramps,' she said, and scraped the sauce off the fish.

Dan had three keys cut, while he waited for three-quarters of an hour. He only strictly needed one key to the side door of the Chestnut Horse, but it was occasionally handy to have spare keys to spare places. You got three keys, per key, cheaper than you got one. It was less of a waste of money than the frozen cod.

Dan left Fred Dawson's van more or less where he had found it. He had used very little petrol, and Fred would get tax relief, and reclaim the VAT on what he had used. He was doing another favour, really – he hated to think of Fred paying more tax than he need.

It was possible that Fred and his wife had never even noticed the absence of the van. It was possible that they had, and that the place was planted out with bluebottles. That was why Dan stopped a little short of his starting point. Fred might notice that the van had mysteriously moved; he might suspect the pixies, or he might suspect Dan. Dan had kept his gloves on throughout, except while paying for the keys.

Fiona knew he had been to Milchester. She could not know how or why. If she later guessed, it would be with astonishment at his ingenuity and resources.

The Chestnut Horse at lunchtime was almost uninhabitable.

Ted Goldingham had got a lift into Milchester, to bank his takings. He had not done any shopping. Ivy had not gone with him. She did not appear in the bar. Somebody was cleaning up the car, in the yard behind the pub.

An unidentified voice advanced the theory, immediately accepted, that Ted had put a pot of paint on a shelf over the garage door. Vibration had wobbled it to the edge, and then over the edge. The word 'vibration' was taken up and repeated, as explaining the whole episode. Examples were produced of the mysterious workings of vibration. It cured, and caused, aches and pains; it moved heavy objects extraordinary distances; it made holes in things.

The fact that there was no shelf over the garage door was overwhelmed by received and accepted wisdom.

How had the paint-can got to the bottom of the garden, then? The answer was easy: kids. Playing truant from school, no proper discipline at home, running wild. There were as many examples of this contemporary scourge as there were of the effects of vibration. Indeed they were compared. The explanation was considered proved by the fact that Ted Goldingham, by his own admission, had not relocked the door of the garage. His distracted state of mind was proved by his having dropped his bunch of keys in the middle of the yard. That was actually because the whole accident with the paint was the result of his own carelessness.

Ted Goldingham was not pleased with his customers.

Dan slipped out towards the Gents', passing the nearly-clean car. The bloke doing the job was having a break in the bar, which was why Dan was there at that moment. Dan borrowed the bunch of keys, which was lying on the driver's seat. In the Gents', he took the anonymous key from the ring and replaced the one to the side door of the pub.

Phase One accomplished, it was time to proceed at once with Phase Two. More balls were to be set rolling, in directions which were to be convincing and attractive. To change the metaphor (Dan realised that changing the metaphor was what he was doing) two pumps, preferably more, had to be primed and set going.

139

The first pump was the Chestnut Horse, and the time to set it going was now. The word 'coincidence' was somehow introduced. It was a small world; everybody agreed about that. For instance, many of the people present had been born *in the same village*, which was Medwell. And take the case of that Mr Potter at the Old Mill. What about him? Was in London the week before the murder. Stale news, everybody knows that. Went to one o' they Soho strip-clubs. Stale, stale, everybody knows that. Saw that Harry Curtis. Yes, o' course, that's one o' the reasons Harry Curtis came to Medwell. But that Terence Barclay moved to Winterbourne – *he* were in London then *too*. Yes, 'course he was. He went to a strip-club. Yes, seem like they all do. Who did *he* see? That Cora Smith, everybody heard that days ago. Who else did he see? Harry Curtis, o' course, along wi' Cora. Who else? Wilfred Potter, likely. If you go to a strip-club, you see other blokes going to a strip-club, stands to reason. No coincidence yet, no small world about it so far. Ah, but who was Harry Curtis with, which both Potter and Barclay saw? Well, who? You'll never guess. Put me out o' my misery. They do say it was Julie Gundry.

Who says such a thing? One o' they 'immen t' post office.

Dan ducked out of the pub, unnoticed in departure as in presence, and primed the pump of the post office.

Within hours each story would meet the other, all over the village, with the result that both would be confirmed.

Dan primed his third pump, by telling Lady Simpson what he had heard in the pub and the post office. By this time Lady Simpson could hear it for herself.

Nobody told Jim Gundry, and conversation in the post office died when Beryl Gundry came in.

There was some sympathy for Jim. An old-fashioned father with a modern daughter. But the strap had had the opposite effect, as it usually did. Julie had probably *boasted* to him, on the telephone from Guildford, about her new American gentleman. Then of course Jim only had to take one look at Harry Curtis . . .

No police cars came for Jim Gundry. Of course they were closing ranks, protecting their own.

In any case, how did Jim get in through that locked door?

The others could have got in – pretty well all the others – because Harry Curtis was expecting them. You didn't lock the door against somebody you were blackmailing. Naturally not – you left it open wide and made them welcome. But Harry Curtis wouldn't have made Jim Gundry welcome, not by a jugful, a policeman and the father of the girl he had seduced.

Speculation concentrated not on whether Jim Gundry had done it, or why he had done it, but simply on how he had got through the side door of the pub.

This was the situation when the Chestnut Horse closed on the night of 4 November.

Guy Fawkes Day, traditionally celebrated in the village the way it was traditionally celebrated in every other village.

The bonfire would be lit at six o'clock, by which time it would be full dark whatever the weather. The fireworks, on Admiral Jenkyn's signal, would start soaring and crackling at about 6.15. The wine cup would begin stickily to flow at some point between these moments, as late, and for as short a time, as the Admiral could contrive. Children were not to be allowed near the fireworks or the wine cup (the Helpers were strictly briefed – there had been one or two shocking cases, in recent years, of tipsy ten-year-olds). The Guy had been made by the children of the village school; from what Dan had seen it was neither better nor worse than all the other Guys of his life. It was hoisted into position at the top of the bonfire by the Cricket Club's part-time groundsman, who deplored the whole thing on account of the threat to his wicket.

At the Calloways' on the morning of the fifth, Dan contrived to get the use of a typewriter. He acquired a small, buff-coloured luggage label, with a piece of string through a re-inforced hole. On the label he typed: SIDE DOOR CH HORSE. He tied the label to one of his new keys. He prematurely aged the label, by wetting it and scrunching it up and dirtying it and drying it, but not so much that the typewritten line was illegible.

In the post office, on his way home, he bought half-a-dozen squibs, saying that they were the only sort of fireworks his mother could be doing with. He left behind a strange picture, of a small and secret firework party, just Dan and his mother, with half-a-dozen squibs jumping about in the edge of the woods by their cottage.

When he left for the cricket pitch at 5.45 he had with him gloves, a disposable plastic cigarette lighter, a pocket flash, the squibs, and the key with the buff-coloured label.

There was already quite a good crowd, when he arrived with his bicycle parked behind the pub. (There had been no sign of Ted Goldingham's car. It had been cleaned up and put away. No lasting harm had been done. Some fellow who needed the work had had a job for the day. Dan was a creator of employment.) It was a fine night, but dark. There was a lantern on the trestle table where the wine cup – not yet – would be dispensed, and another on a table where somebody was selling tickets for something. Beams swung to and fro, like searchlights in a film about the war, as people made last-minute inspections of bonfire, Guy, and fireworks. There were lights in the cricket pavilion, fifty yards away, where members of the Club Committee were having better drinks than the wine cup. Somebody had brought the drinks in a basket – leaving bottles overnight, in a locked cupboard, had been an expensive and unrepeated experiment. Dan would not have been allowed in. He did not want to go in. He wanted to locate Jim Gundry, and then to be his shadow. (Poor Jim. Nobody had yet had the heart to talk to him and Beryl about Julie. It would all come out at the trial.)

There would be a lot more light when they put a match to the bonfire, but there would be deep shadows too. Dan wanted both.

Jim was certain to be there, officially, to prevent arson and over-excitement. Even in the dark he was casting his usual gloom. Dan was glad to see that he was wearing his uniform mackintosh. It made his pockets easier to get at, not for abstraction but for insertion.

Dan was anxious that his squibs should not ignite prematurely, in his pocket. That would destroy his plan and probably his trousers.

Nothing was happening yet. Heartiness prevailed. Faces loomed in and out of the localised glow of the lanterns, or were fleetingly illuminated by the waving beams. Dan saw the Reverend Gordon Hedges, busy at the edge of the bonfire. He saw Mrs Hedges, in a group of people, trying to look as though she was all right. He saw the Jenkyns, the Calloways, the Blacks and Mrs Potter. Terence Barclay and Wilfred Potter were no doubt drinking whisky in the cricket pavilion. Between them, there might be a powerful atmosphere, socially.

Dan saw Mrs Cora Smith, talking to somebody and looking like a child on its birthday. Her hair was fluffed round a beret, and she had a long scarf thrown over her shoulder. She looked impossibly wholesome.

Dan saw the Muspratts. Fiona was bareheaded. She was smiling; she was beautiful. She was looking round in the intermittent darkness, looking for someone. She might be looking for Dan; she might be looking for Francis Morley. Francis Morley probably deserved such a girl. Dan didn't. Well, he had not got such a girl.

Dan saw Terence Barclay, emerged from the whisky fumes of the cricket pavilion. Once again, he seemed to have left his wife at home; perhaps fireworks gave her a migraine. He was also looking for someone. Dan knew who he was looking for. No doubt he would find her, or she him.

People shouted, and other people told them to keep quiet. Admiral Jenkyn adopted a quarterdeck manner. The bonfire was simultaneously lit at several points, amid ritual cheers. The flames began to gobble the dry brushwood, licking up towards the Guy. The crackle drowned all ordinary conversation. Paraffin and diesel oil had been poured on to the bonfire, and some of the wood had been treated with tar or creosote. Fingers of flame towered momentarily far above the Guy. Light and shade became dramatic, lurid, like a vision of a cheerful hell.

Admiral Jenkyn, with apparent reluctance but yielding to democratic pressure, gave the signal for the wine cup to be dispensed. The tureen was uncovered and the ladle wielded over a ready regiment of plastic cups. The spicy smell of the wine cup mingled pleasantly with the aromatic smells of tar and fruitwood from the bonfire.

Jim Gundry glanced keenly this way and that, making sure

that nobody got up to any mischief. Somebody offered him some wine cup, but he never drank on duty.

Admiral Jenkyn had a sheet of paper on a clip-board, instructions to himself, Orders of the Day, Fireworks, Sequence of Ignition of. He had a whistle in his mouth and a flashlight in his hand. A blast from his whistle was followed by the successive whooshes of a battery of rockets. *Ooh* and *Aah*. Roman candles, and Catherine-wheels on fence posts. Two of six Catherine-wheels stuck; one, prodded by the Scoutmaster with a stick to get it going, fell off into the grass, where it lay spitting and popping in humiliation. Children waved sparklers, spiralling or spelling out rude words. Larky spirits lit squibs, which jumped noisily about among the crowd, causing people to scream and tread on one another's toes.

Dan camouflaged himself as one of the crowd, jumping and shrieking; he kept his head low and his face in shadow. Shrunk to the size of a ten-year-old, he materialised immediately behind Jim Gundry. The crowd eddied round. The fire roared, the fireworks went crack-crack-crack, bass and treble voices were raised against the other noises. Dan took the key with the tag out of his pocket; he held the key in his teeth, so that the label hung down his chin like a semi-severed tongue. He took out a squib and the cigarette lighter. Gloved, he had some difficulty working the lighter. He lit the touch-paper of the squib. He pocketed the lighter, at the same time blundering into the back of Jim Gundry. He took the key out of his mouth and posted it into Jim's mackintosh pocket, followed by the lit squib. Nobody saw him doing any of these things; or if anybody saw them being done, they did not see who did them.

Dan withdrew, still shrunk and faceless, into an anonymous gobbet of the crowd, a yard and a half from Jim Gundry. He took out his flashlight.

The first bang of the squib, hardly muffled by the material of Jim's coat, went off most unexpectedly four feet above the ground. Jim jumped about four feet off the ground, at the same time beating at his right hip and then peeling off the mackintosh. He jumped up and down on the mackintosh, his huge boots undoubtedly extinguishing the squib.

Dan switched on his flashlight. Holding it at arm's length, he trained the beam on the mackintosh, on the pocket where the squib was. Other beams were trained there and thereabouts and on Jim Gundry, but Dan kept his pinned to that pocket.

It was inevitable that Jim should pull the dead squib out of the pocket. It was inevitable that he should examine at once the outside and inside of the coat for damage, and then the lining of the pocket. The beam of Dan's flashlight reliably helped him, as other beams unreliably did. As he pulled the pocket inside out he revealed the label and then the key.

Jim exclaimed at the sight of the key, producing not so much a word as a noise from farmyard or forest. He was either surprised to see the key coming out of his pocket, or he was simulating surprise. It was difficult to hear what he said, if he said anything, because of the noise of the bonfire and the fireworks and the crowd, only a dozen of whom were aware of the outrage in Jim Gundry's pocket.

Jim stooped to pick up the luggage tag, from which dangled the key. It seemed to Dan that the tag had been singed; it had certainly not been consumed. Jim held the tag close to his eyes. He peered at it, assisted by the light of half-a-dozen wavering torches and of Dan's, which had travelled with it and remained pinpointed on it. The label was blank. Jim was looking at the wrong side. Anybody would have turned the label over, and at long, long last Jim did so. Torch-beams crowded in. Dan's was no longer necessary. He switched it off, and ducked to the level of the smallest children.

'Side door cher 'orse,' read Jim, loud enough to be heard over the ambient clamour.

Then that happened which Dan had not dared hope for. Throughout the operation he had, it seemed to him, been bucking odds consistently stacked against him, overcoming them by dint of audacity and ingenuity. He had not really had one single stroke of luck. Now he had one, not before time. ''Ere,' came Ted Goldingham's voice out of the darkness, 'what the ruddy 'ell are you doin' wi' my key?'

In the presence of a considerable crowd, the key was tried in the side door of the Chestnut Horse. The scene was lit by the rump of the fireworks, exploding overhead; the hot-orange glow of the declining bonfire plunged the alley into deepest blackness.

To Dan, imperceptible at the fringe of the crowd, Jim Gundry was visibly nonplussed. He did not know how he had come by the key. It had not come out of his pocket. Somebody had planted it on him.

'Wunner o'w long Jim 'ad 'at key?' piped a senile voice at the edge of the crowd.

Dan, having made the remark in a fair imitation of his mother's voice, moved undetected to another part of the alley.

All about him, the penny dropped. Look at 'at label on 'at key. Bin around for months, maybe years. 'At's 'ow Jim Gundry got t' Curtis. Jim's own knife, likely, took off a villain when 'e were arresten 'un. No blamen Jim, wi' Julie an' all, but murder's murder, no getten round 'at.

Nobody knew how to proceed, the situation being unprecedented. Dan crept away while the village debated it.

Dan was sure that Terence Barclay would by this time have located and removed Cora Smith, and taken her away in his car to wherever they went. Their first meeting had been pretty quick, but their subsequent sessions were probably slower. They could both say later, if asked, that they had been to the bonfire, and people would remember seeing them there.

The Jim Gundry episode had been triumphantly successful, and none of it added up to a row of beans. It took the eye of the village off the ball, but it would not distract the detectives in Milchester.

Dan decided that there was a new and optimum account of the events of the night of the murder, and that he would make it come to have been true. Thus:

Cora Smith was a tart and Harry Curtis her protector. Either one of them, or both, made a quick and tactful deal with the all-too-willing Terence Barclay. He faded away from the Church Rooms, followed Cora Smith and found, of course, that the side door of the pub had been left unlocked for him. Up he goes, hoppity-hop to her bedroom, where she's waiting for him. He probably gets less than his money's-worth, on account of being pushed for time, but there's a promise of more later. Harry Curtis is next door throughout, knowing what's going on, probably having arranged it, certainly getting his cut. He invites Terence Barclay to contribute very much more than Cora's fee, first thing next day, or Mrs Barclay and the rest of the world will know that Terence went straight from church to a tart's bedroom over the pub. Terence Barclay gargles his consent, nips downstairs, comes casually out of the alley (the bit Dan actually saw) and rejoins the party. Having told lies all his life, he can easily summon up one or two more.

Terence then equips himself with a knife. He goes out of the side door of the Church Rooms, fetches a considerable compass, gets to the cricket field, goes through Enid and Bob Cranston's garden, and comes back to the side door of the pub, which is still unlocked. He may just about coincide with Sandra Hedges; he may hear her voice from the stairs; he may arrive after she's left. Cora Smith also leaves: conceivably Terence sends her away. Terence is fit for his age, and pretty desperate. He does what he came to do, leaving the knife behind with Harry Curtis's prints on it. He goes home to his wife, and makes her migraine worse by saying what a nice party they had in the Church Rooms, and how many of their neighbours he chatted with.

Of course Cora Smith knew he had done it. She was probably pleased. She might have *asked* him to do it. Now she was blackmailing him, and he was blackmailing her, so they were quits. Very cosy. She might never go back to Nebraska.

Back on the cricket field, Dan looked at the glowing pile of ash surrounded by the husks of dead fireworks. He examined the new revelation. He found it wonderfully convincing. He did not see how anybody could fail to believe it. The bit that could be exposed, as a pointer to all the rest, was Terence Barclay's carry-on with Cora Smith. The rest might be difficult to prove, but that bit would be easy. It involved a bit of creeping and peeping, possibly distasteful, but you could find anything if you knew what you were looking for and you knew it was there.

Dan circled the dark edge of the cricket field, not wishing his face to be seen while the ridiculous fuss about Jim Gundry was still going on. He stumbled against something on the ground. An old coat. A new coat. A dummy. A body. A dead body. A man's dead body.

Dan winked his pocket flash. It was Terence Barclay. He had been shot in the back at a range close enough for the powder to have singed his covert-coat.

Of course the gun had been fired in the middle of the fireworks – the shot would have been lost in the bang-bang-bang of rockets and squibs and Roman candles. Everybody would have an alibi and nobody would have one. Most people were wearing gloves, on a chilly November evening.

Motive? Dan knew who had killed Terence Barclay and why. The implications were as horrible as could be.

Dan felt bad about leaving the body to the field-mice, but worse about reporting it to Jim Gundry. He found his bicycle, went home, and had a whisky and water.

He found the five remaining squibs in his trouser pocket. He let them off, one by one, at the edge of the wood, while his mother watched from the kitchen window. He was not in a mood for letting off fireworks, but his mother demanded it. She would have preferred rockets. The dogs thought somebody was shooting, and moaned with excitement. It was an intimate domestic end to a complicated day.

II

The body was found at first light.

It was thought for a time that the unfortunate gentleman had been hit by a wayward firework.

It was considered odd that Mrs Barclay had not reported her husband missing, at eleven o'clock or at midnight; it became obvious that he had often been missing at those hours and later.

The bullet came from a .38 revolver.

The revolver was found by a metal detector, in long grass at the edge of the field, near the gate into the Cranstons' garden. The Cranstons thought it a liberty, dumping a murder weapon near their gate. The gun was a Smith and Wesson short-barrelled Special, American, about thirty years old but in good condition. It was a kind of gun readily available in large numbers, at a moderate price, all over the world. One chamber only had been fired; there were three more rounds in the cylinder. There were no fingerprints on butt, trigger, trigger-guard or cylinder, but there were prints on the stubby barrel. The fingerprints were those of the late Harry Curtis.

Mrs Cora Smith had never seen the gun. She gave a little scream when she was shown it. She did not know that Harry Curtis had had a gun. She had no idea whether Harry Curtis had brought it to Europe or acquired it in Britain.

Mrs Smith had met Mrs Barclay, at coffee mornings in the village, but she did not think she had ever met the deceased. She expressed her sympathy for the widow, having herself been recently bereaved far away in America, and having lost a kinsman the previous month, small loss though that turned out to be, which in a way made it worse, did the Chief Superintendent know what she meant?

The police expected an early arrest. 'They would, wouldn't they?' said the village in pub and post office.

The new tragedy swamped public interest in the outrages to Ted Goldingham's car and Jim Gundry's mackintosh, but not the interest of the two victims. United as never before, they attacked Dan Mallett.

Dan blankly denied that he had done any of the things they said he had done, in relation to vandalising cars, causing explosions in pockets, or murdering Terence Barclay. He said that he had not been near any of those places; at the relevant times he had been getting his mother's breakfast, dinner or tea, and letting off his mother's fireworks. He appealed to his mother for confirmation. She cackled at the police, incoherent, demented. They left at last in frustrated exhaustion, which was the effect she always had on them.

'Rum doens,' she said afterwards to Dan. 'Why did ye seek t' paint 'at bloke's car?'

Dan's story was corroborated, bizarrely enough, by the little corpses of dead squibs found at the edge of the wood near his cottage.

Ted Goldingham was reluctant to serve Dan, and Jim Gundry looked at him darkly. These things were nothing new. Ted had always said that Dan lowered the tone of the Chestnut Horse, and Jim that he was the biggest villain unhung.

Francis Morley came again to stay, as he had promised, with his cousins. Lady Simpson was full of it.

On the Saturday after the Thursday of Guy Fawkes night, he arrived at the Muspratts' in his BMW and took Fiona out to dinner. He took her to the Old Mill. Lady Simpson, on Monday, was full of it. She said Sir George said he could not afford dinner at the Old Mill.

Mrs Sandra Hedges was arrested on Tuesday morning, having been cautioned and charged, in front of witnesses, for the murder of Harry Curtis and Terence Barclay.

'They found out in Nebraska that Sandra was married

before,' said Mrs Jenkyn to Lady Simpson. 'She was married to Harry Curtis. They don't seem to know if she was ever divorced.'

The ladies supposed Dan to be drinking hot sweet tea in the Simpsons' kitchen, at the other end of the house.

'And Terence Barclay gave a sealed letter to his lawyer,' went on Mrs Jenkyn, 'saying it should be opened if anything happened to him. The letter said that, although he was not there at the time, he knew who had murdered Harry Curtis, and the murderer knew that he knew. Of course he meant poor Sandra.'

'If he knew such a thing, why ever didn't he tell the police?' said Lady Simpson.

'They say that he liked exercising power. He was holding it over Sandra's head. There's no knowing what he would have done to her in the long run.'

Dan thought Mrs Jenkyn knew quite well what Terence Barclay's long-term plans for Sandra were, and Lady Simpson did too.

'The poor little thing collapsed,' said Mrs Jenkyn. 'She couldn't or wouldn't tell them anything about it. It was a dreadful thing to have seen. One felt so powerless to help. There was a policewoman who was worried about her, about her and the baby. They've taken her into hospital, but she's still under arrest.'

'That poor baby . . .'

'The baby will be born, if it is, while she's remanded in custody awaiting trial. Gordon Hedges was like a sleepwalker. He didn't take in anything anybody said. He kept bumping into things. I would have been worried for the Waterford, if my mind had been on such things . . . He went with her, with some clothes. We don't know where he is now. The only thing he said was that he was going to resign.'

'He can't have known about any of it,' said Lady Simpson.

'No, of course not,' said Mrs Jenkyn. 'Even if he thought she was divorced, he would never have married her in church.'

'How did they discover about the other marriage? Why didn't the duffers find out weeks ago?'

'We don't know,' said Mrs Jenkyn. 'Things are evidently

different in America. It was simply a piece of paper that got lost. Marriage, divorce, they seem to make nothing of it. And it seems from the police over there that they didn't live anywhere as man and wife, in a house of their own, as the rest of us do, as part of a community, paying taxes and so forth. They were on no electoral register or anything of the kind.'

'They simply went from hotel to hotel?'

'"Motels" I think would be the word.'

'What a dreadful way to live,' said Lady Simpson. 'Expensive, too. I suppose he was making a dishonest living in various ways. It seems he was still doing so, when he came here. He came to blackmail poor little Sandra. Oh dear oh dear. However did he know about the Hedges, about their marriage, about them coming here?'

'It was an article in an American magazine,' said Mrs Jenkyn. 'The Hedges have a copy. They showed it to us, when they first came here.'

'I remember,' said Lady Simpson. 'Indeed, indeed.'

'The dreadful Harry Curtis picked up the magazine, saw a picture of his wife marrying a Church of England parson, read the name Medwell, packed a suitcase with his knife and his pistol . . . Why did he bring little Cora Smith along? On a business trip? When he was going to commit a horrible crime?'

'She says she doesn't know.'

'I know she says she doesn't know.'

Both ladies were silent for a moment, contemplating (like Ivy Goldingham) the scarcely credible innocence of Cora Smith.

'The police must know that Gordon Hedges has been lying to them,' said Lady Simpson at last. 'He says he was awake half the night, and they were in the same bedroom.'

'Nobody is going to blame him for that,' said Mrs Jenkyn.

'No, but an ordained minister . . .'

'And apparently they cannot oblige him to give evidence for the prosecution.'

'Leaving aside his feelings,' said Lady Simpson, 'it is a difficult position for him.'

Dan thought this the understatement of a lifetime; he knew that Mrs Jenkyn's and Lady Simpson's sympathy was genuine.

Both their husbands had been fleetingly suspected, in pub and post office, of the first murder. In point of opportunity, they might equally have been suspected of the second, as might Wilfred Potter, Ted Goldingham, Jim Gundry or Dan himself. The time for such diversions was past. It was now time for despair.

'The poor boy's position is impossible,' said Mrs Jenkyn, 'which is why he's resigning the living. That's the one thing he did say, before they all left.'

'*What* a loss to the parish,' said Lady Simpson. 'I imagine him going abroad, don't you – Central Africa or some such, where nobody has ever heard of them and everybody is too desperate to care . . .'

'He will not go away,' said Mrs Jenkyn, 'as long as he can help her.'

'But, my dear, how can he help her?'

'By holding her hand. She is having a baby in two weeks.'

Dan thought this an excellent reply. Mrs Jenkyn had risen, and was rising still, in his estimation.

'We think she did not go there intending to kill him,' said Mrs Jenkyn presently. 'We imagine he laughed at her, and demanded thousands and thousands of pounds . . . Perhaps she knew about that knife, where he would have kept it in the room . . .'

Dan nodded to his reflection in the glass-fronted bookcase in the Simpsons' hall. What Mrs Jenkyn was saying was all, as far as he knew, exactly right.

Lady Simpson unexpectedly said, 'What should she have said to him – what should Sandra have said to Gordon – when they first met?'

'When they very first met?' said Mrs Jenkyn. 'It was at a concert, as you recall. Everybody knows that. It was mentioned in the magazine. What should she have said? What would anybody say, to a stranger, at a concert, about their marital status?'

'There must have come a moment . . .' said Lady Simpson.

'Yes, dear, but that kind of moment is past before you realise it has arrived.'

Dan thought that here, too, Mrs Jenkyn was exactly right.

153

You realised too late. About nearly everything, nearly every-body realised too late.

Sandra had realised, too late, that Gordon's feelings were really strong, and that her own were really strong, and that by telling the truth she would be putting a bomb under two people, wrecking two lives . . . Sandra recognised that her happiness depended on Gordon, and that his happiness depended on her. She kept quiet for his sake as much as her own. She was living a lie, for his sake as much as her own.

'There is a point in the marriage service,' said Lady Simpson slowly, 'at which the officiating clergyman says – in this case the Bishop himself said – "I require and charge you both, as ye will answer at the dreadful day of judgement when – ah –"'

'"The secrets of all hearts shall be disclosed,"' said Mrs Jenkyn.

'Yes yes yes. "If either of you know any impediment why ye may not be lawfully joined together in matrimony . . ."'

'"You do now confess it." Yes, dear, but was Sandra sup-posed to pipe up, in the middle of the cathedral, in front of the Bishop?'

'Yes,' said Lady Simpson.

Dan was not so sure. It sounded to him, by the fact of her silence, that Mrs Jenkyn was not so sure either.

Sandra had weighed her immortal soul against Gordon's happiness, and it was no contest. She sacrificed her peace of mind and her hope of heaven for his happiness. She would believe that that was what she was doing. Her first marriage did not exist. It meant nothing to her. It was a bad dream, out of sight, the other side of the world, something that had not happened.

'Why ever,' said Lady Simpson, picking up Dan's thoughts as though on cue (which was not surprising, as they were all thinking about the same thing), 'why ever did a sweet girl like Sandra marry a man as odious as that?'

'I know her very well, after all these weeks,' said Mrs Jenkyn, 'and I think I can explain that. She was very young, you know, very ignorant and innocent, and brought up by dreadfully strict, intolerant relatives. We have heard much about her childhood and youth. It is difficult for us to imagine. Our children went away to school, they have lived in London and travelled – she had never been anywhere or met anybody, or lived in a place larger than this village . . . What afflicts me is that the discovery of that first marriage was simply inevitable. She must have been living with that knowledge.'

And with Terence Barclay's knowledge of that knowledge, thought Dan.

Dan heard the clink of cups being replaced on saucers, and the twanging of springs as armchairs were relieved of the weights of the ladies. He trotted back to the kitchen, and emptied Lady Simpson's idea of a working man's tea down the sink.

Dan had always known, all along, exactly what had happened on the night of the first murder. There were unanswered questions, a lot of them, but a dismally clear answer to the big one. Now he knew the reason, and it was the kind of reason that had suggested itself from the very beginning, to himself and to everybody else. 'Can't be a coincidence,' everybody had said. 'Matter o' simple common sense.' It couldn't be a coincidence, and it wasn't, and it was a matter of simple common sense. The plot had kept thickening, of its own daft momentum and with Dan's help – wild geese, red herrings, flashy watches in gardens, white-haired blokes dodging behind trees, all sorts of people having been to America, conversations that happened or didn't in the Church Rooms, Ted Goldingham, Jim Gundry – which had taken everybody's eyes, for a moment or two, off the central fact. Now they were back there again, and there they'd stay.

The most obvious explanations – the first that came into your head – probably answered all those silly questions of the fringes. Somebody nobody ever heard of – some tripper in the summer – had dropped that watch in Vince Mellins's garden. It was the sort of watch you could go swimming with. A few weeks of fine weather, in the thick shelter of Vince's weeds, would have done it no harm. A tramp with white hair wanted to relieve himself, late at night, on the roadside between the village and the Jenkyns'; naturally he skipped behind a tree – anybody would, caught at such a moment. And so forth and so forth. There might never be final answers to any of these questions, and it didn't make a bit of difference.

Dan wondered how people would react. Successive theories, more or less ridiculous, had marched across the sky over the village like clouds of war, or visitations of plague, or advertisement banners towed by light aircraft. Each theory had produced an absolute polarity of response. Dan had known, from Lady Simpson and Mrs Calloway and Fiona, how the nobs had reacted in each case; he had known from the post office and the Chestnut Horse how the village had reacted.

Now there seemed to be no reaction at all. More thoroughly examined, people were so shocked, so numbed, that nobody said anything, except to mumble sympathy for the Reverend Gordon Hedges.

The Vicar himself was unseen. He packed up and left the Jenkyns', to save them and himself embarrassment. He was known to have written to the Bishop and to have seen lawyers. He was assumed to be living, as anonymously as possible, in some sort of lodgings in Milchester. Nobody knew where Mrs Hedges was, either, except that she was in a bed in a hospital where she belonged, and they said the imminent baby seemed to be all right.

A local lay reader, a lugubrious stockbroker of aggressive piety, took over some of the Vicar's duties, pending yet another appointment, yet another Service of Induction. The old Vicar was dragged out of retirement for Sunday and midweek Communion. The life of the parish went on. The life of the village would have gone on, for all but a tiny minority, whether the church had been functioning or not. The village needed the post office and the Chestnut Horse, but only a few old ladies truly needed the church. This thought was half uttered in, such profane places as the workshop behind Cribbin's Garage; it was not voiced in the houses of Sir George Simpson or Admiral Jenkyn.

Mrs Monica Barclay was astonishingly brave about the shocking death of her husband. People said she was bearing up wonderfully. She said she would move back to London. The house would be put on the market in the spring.

Mrs Cora Smith continued popular among the golf-widows of insurance brokers, who made her a kind of pet, or mascot.

Dan wondered why he had not seen her running out of the Chestnut Horse after Gordon Hedges. He wondered how she had known which way to run.

The answers to both questions were obvious. The moment he arrived, Harry Curtis would have found out where the Hedges were staying. He only had to ask. Nobody would remember question or answer. There were still maybe two hours of daylight when Harry Curtis and Cora Smith arrived in Medwell. It was a fine evening, warm for the time of year. They went for a stroll. Anybody would. It would be extraordinary not to look round a place you had travelled so far to see. Probably they went out frontwards, up the street, saw the lovingly restored cottages, the fine old church, the ancient graveyard with yews and pollarded lime trees. And they went out backwards, into the yard, saw what had been stables and barn, saw the way out through the Granstons' garden to the cricket pitch, saw that you could reach the Jenkyns' that way, and sit and wait for somebody coming the ordinary way . . .

Cora had planned in advance to waylay Gordon Hedges? Why? Did she know in advance that Terence Barclay was coming to bed her, that Sandra was going to kill Harry?

Something was completely wrong. Dan pondered the events of the night of the first murder.

Not long after Gordon Hedges got home – possibly even before he did – Sandra Hedges slipped out of the Jenkyns' house to keep her appointment with Harry Curtis. Gordon Hedges let her go. Would he? Would anybody be that apathetic, that trusting? Wouldn't he follow her? It might strike him as a distasteful thing to do, almost spying on his own wife, but he'd surely feel obliged to keep an eye on her, protect her from whatever she was running into.

If he followed her, why didn't Dan see him? Oh Lord, how dim, how slow, how stupid. Dan didn't see Gordon Hedges, but he was aware of his presence, there by the churchyard, watching as Dan was watching. And when Sandra went home again he followed her. And *then* he was intercepted by Cora Smith.

Figures moved and paused and moved over the dark landscape, in Dan's mind.

Cora Smith was not lurking in any ditch, waiting for Gordon Hedges. She was sitting in the dark in her bedroom, having got rid of her visitor, waiting for Harry Curtis to have his visitor. How did she know he was going to have a visitor? Did he tell her? The visitor came. Threats, mockery, despair. 'All right, honey, I dare you – here's my back and here's my knife, and you won't have the guts to do it.' Something like that.

Sandra wiped the knife and then searched the room. Anything with her name, diaries, addresses, photocopies of documents about that first marriage. It was conceivable that Harry Curtis had left such things in a bank, or a hotel safe, or the luggage office of a railway station. It was much more likely that he had them with him, and that they went on to the Jenkyns' incinerator early the following morning.

Sandra left. Cora followed. She went by the back way, so that she was quite certain not to be seen. She was quite certain of catching Sandra before Sandra reached the Jenkyns'. But instead of catching Sandra she caught Gordon. Yes, inevitably, because Gordon was between Sandra and Cora. She expected to talk to Sandra; she talked to Gordon instead.

No doubt the police now had confirmation from Cora Smith, and possibly Gordon Hedges, about all the events of that night. Gordon Hedges couldn't be made to give evidence against his wife, but Cora Smith could. The American Embassy would tell her to tell the exact truth, and so would the police and all the lawyers and any minister of religion she consulted. Probably nobody in the world except Dan would actually advise her to commit perjury; and if she did she couldn't say it hadn't happened, only that she didn't know what had happened.

It might be difficult to prove that Sandra killed Terence Barclay, with the gun she had taken from Harry Curtis's bedroom after she had killed him. But Terence said he knew who Harry's murderer was, so whoever murdered Harry murdered Terence too. Anyway, the Prosecution didn't have to prove two murders. One did the trick.

Dan was glad the death penalty had been abolished, but he wondered if Sandra Hedges was.

Woodbines, the Calloways' house, was pretentious and over-decorated, like many of the nobs' and near-nobs' places in the neighbourhood. (The Jenkyns' house was an exception.) Dan knew them all, some better than others. None of them, except the Jenkyns', had been left as it was; all of them had been mucked about and tarted up, nearly all in the previous dozen years. Dan had made varying contributions to the mucking and tarting processes, sometimes acting as a kind of broker of constructional or decorative bits and pieces – of mantelpieces, shelving, panels, shutters, oddments of stone and wrought iron. He had produced the massive bracket from which hung the light over the Potters' door; he was coy to the Potters about its origin, because it had been in the old stables of the Chestnut Horse. He had produced the sitting-room door for the Calloways, who wanted a nice old-fashioned solid one; he had been coy about that, too, because it had come from the Potters' garden shed. The Calloways had painted the door a horrible mustard one side and a horrible orange the other, but it was a solid old bit of oak planking.

Dan was reminded about that door when he was painting the skirting-boards in the Calloways' hall. Mildred Calloway was on the other side of the door, in the sitting-room, telephoning. Dan knew she was telephoning because he had heard the bell of the extension in the kitchen. Then he had heard her voice, quite close to the door on the other side. He could hear that there was a voice; he would not have known that it was her voice, and he could certainly not hear what she said.

Doors. He thought of the ones in his own cottage, none of which was even approximately rectangular. The lofty, polished, brass-laden doors of Medwell Court. The folksy pine of some of the renovated cottages in the village. The plywood panels put in by the builders who had turned the Monk's House into flats. You could hear a housefly cleaning its wings through one of them. One thing on the credit side for the Calloways – perhaps the only thing, but positive as far as it went – they had insisted on this excellent door.

It was a quiet day, windless, drizzling. Dan ought to have been raking up the sodden leaves on the Calloways' lawn, but he had managed to persuade Mrs Calloway that she could not for another day endure the scuff-marks and stains on the skirting-boards in the hall. It was a job to take slowly. If you hurried it you sloshed paint on the wall and floor. The gloss paint had a penetrating smell, quite different from that of the emulsion paint which had somehow got spread on Ted Goldingham's car.

There was another bloke who liked good doors, even if he had no other notions of good taste. Dan laid down his paintbrush, carefully, on the lid of the can, and sat back on his heels; he listened to the distant murmur which was all he could make out of Mrs Calloway's voice. You wouldn't hear any more through any of the doors in that pub . . .

You wouldn't hear any more, from one bedroom to another, if the door between them was shut.

Dan picked up the brush, and absently painted a square foot of the wall.

Harry Curtis had known – yes, must have known – that Cora Smith had left the party in the Church Rooms, had gone into the pub and upstairs to her bedroom. He went soon afterwards, leaving the outside door on the latch for Cora's new client and for Sandra Hedges. Waiting for Sandra in his room, he knew that Cora Smith was next door, with Terence Barclay and then without him.

Was the door open or shut?

If it was shut, there was no way Cora could have heard the conversation in Harry's room, no way she could have known who his visitor was unless she had known in advance. She could only have known in advance if he had told her, if she was a party to the whole horrible scheme.

If it was open, even a crack, Harry would have known that it was and been content that it was – content that Cora Smith heard everything. She was a party to his blackmail as he was to her prostitution.

Dan painted another square foot of wallpaper, and wondered if his new discovery made any difference. It put Cora Smith in a still more horrible light, but did *that* make any difference? The police were not terribly likely to try to pin on her a charge of abetting blackmail; in the absence of any documents, of any evidence at all, they would never make it stick. Presumably they had done the sum about the door, long before Dan had thought of it, and had tried listening to a conversation through it. It might put Cora Smith's evidence in doubt – depending on what her evidence was, which Dan had no way of knowing – but did the Prosecution need her evidence?

A pussy-cat, a kitten, fluffy and playful. Adopted as a pet by insurance brokers' wives in renovated cottages. Adopted whether he liked it or not, and he probably liked it, by Terence Barclay. By now, Dan imagined, she had a new gentleman, and came and went in another Jaguar from Amy Crate's cottage.

Kittens grew into cats. There had been a marmalade cat loosely attached to his own cottage, until it was found guilty of murdering blue-marble bantam chicks.

One thing which had never been considered, by anybody, was that Harry Curtis was murdered by Cora Smith. Of course it hadn't. She was far away at the time, pouring out something to the Reverend Gordon Hedges. That was immediately after the Vicar had left the party, and long before the murder. But it was now obvious to Dan (in defiance of the evidence and of common sense) that that emotional and confidential conversation had happened during the second, and quite separate, expedition made by the Vicar to the village. For the actual time of the murder, Cora Smith's alibi was completely phoney. Gordon Hedges had known that, perfectly well, all along. So why hadn't he said so?

Because in saying so he was running his own wife's head into the noose, not Cora Smith's head. The person he had supposed to be his wife. Cora Smith had him over a barrel. It was just as much blackmail as the sort Harry Curtis had tried, and much more successful.

Why didn't Cora Smith come out and accuse Sandra Hedges?

Because she couldn't have known who Sandra was, why she came to the Chestnut Horse all alone in the middle of the night, unless she was completely in Harry Curtis's confidence. Either she knew in advance what Harry Curtis was going to say, and to whom and why, or the door between the bedrooms was open.

Dan found he had thus thought himself round in a circle, and further convinced himself of the obvious – Sandra Hedges had acted in panic and despair to get rid of one blackmailer, and then done so again to get rid of another.

Abstractedly, Dan spread another area of white gloss paint over the duck-egg blue wallpaper of the hall.

'Dan!' shrieked a voice behind him, startling him so that he dropped his paint-laden brush on the pastel luxury of the wall-to-wall Wilton broadloom.

Mildred Calloway had finished telephoning, and opened the sitting-room door. Her shriek was that of a woman whose instructions have been exceeded. She moaned at the sight of the paint on the wall; she had not yet seen that on the carpet.

Dan tried to bow humbly, but found it impossible from a squatting position.

'People have been saying you've gone mad,' said Mrs Calloway. 'Everybody's beginning to say so. I've been standing up for you. And *now*, oh dear oh dear oh dear . . .'

Dan got out of the house somehow, out into the clammy drizzle. He thought it unlikely that he would go back inside again, at least with the Calloways' knowledge.

He found that he was holding his cap, so he put it on. He found that the hand that was holding the cap was also holding the paintbrush, which some instinct of decency had made him pick up from the Wilton carpet. He wondered how much paint he had put on his cap, his hair and his forehead.

If everybody thought he was mad he might as well look mad, like an undersized Indian brave or a traditional clown. He supposed Ted Goldingham had been putting it about that he had stepped over the edge into lunacy; Jim Gundry might be saying the same sort of thing.

The paintbrush was Edwin Calloway's property. If Dan went

off with it, Edwin Calloway would claim on his insurance. It would be quite inconvenient to ride a bicycle while holding a paintbrush. Dan put the brush in the Calloways' garden shed. He wondered about putting himself there, until the drizzle stopped; but he concluded that the drizzle would not stop until about Easter.

Dan realised how miserably preoccupied he had been, to go putting a lot of paint on the wrong target. He supposed the Calloways would repaper the wall, Edwin Calloway having claimed on his insurance. He mildly regretted that he would not be doing the job. He charged more for decorating than for gardening, on account of the high degree of skill and concentration required. He usually got his employer to do most of the work.

Martinmas. The weather cleared, for St Martin's summer. The sky was not blue but white, and the country not green but amber. Twigs spidered across the sky, which lately had impaled cushions of green, but suddenly the trees showed that they were by no means bare, but splashed, as though painted by Dan in a mood of abstraction, with yellows and reds; near at hand they looked like dowagers clinging to the remnants of savage magnificence; in the distance they glowed, as though inside each were the warm light of an oil-lamp. In the morning a golden muslin veiled the water-meadows, out of which rose rootless trees and houses without foundations; in the evening it was a pearly blanket, cooler by many degrees than the air on higher ground.

Many birds celebrated, as though bamboozled by unseasonable wet warmth. People said they were remembering summer; Dan was sure they were anticipating spring, by means that sounded lyrical but were actually military – robins, thrushes, wrens were assertively beating the bounds of the territories in which, five months later, they would set up house. They might even be taking their partners for the sexy dances of April.

Sandra Hedges, at the end of quiet, high-security corridors, would hear no birdsong, but only the squeak of rubber soles on hygienic floors.

Then, in the night, there was a great crying of the owls in the dripping Priory Woods behind Dan's cottage. He heard them not from his bed, but on his way to work at two in the morning and his way back at seven in the morning. He was sure his father and his grandfather had been right – the owls were warning anybody who had the sense to be awake and listening that the weather was about to change. When November owls made such a clamour, in the benevolent midst of St Martin's summer, it was time to get your biggest rubber boots out of their estivation in the cupboard under the stairs.

The owls were right. Rain followed rain; if it stopped it was only to gather its forces, as though celestial cisterns were being topped up. The river filled and spilled and darkened, white flecks of foam on chocolate brown, so that it resembled the sort of pudding Dan's mother had once liked. The remaining leaves came down with a rush, and all the earthworms rose to the surface, so that the lawns Dan raked were boggy wastes of compost. The birds took shelter in the bottoms of hedges, and Dan in potting-sheds and greenhouses.

Sandra Hedges would be warm and dry, and given nourishing prenatal food. She would ache to be with the bedraggled finches under the hornbeams; and Gordon Hedges would be sicker at heart than anybody Dan ever heard of.

After two and a half days, the rain relented and the wind dropped, half revealing a world which seemed that it would never be dry again. A watery sun pulled out of the ground a wet mist that took all the colour out of the world.

There was no colour in Dan's world. He could not get the Hedges out of his mind. He did not see Fiona. She was away, abroad, in the South, with friends. Francis Morley was in the party, taking some extra holiday he was owed. They were with two other couples; they were one of the couples in the party. Lady Simpson, talking about them, looked as though she wanted to wink. She expected the engagement to be announced when they got back. Fiona had not said goodbye to Dan, and he did not think she would say hallo.

Dan's mother was aware of his depression, and it depressed her. He did not think she was aware of the reasons, although she might be guessing a part of them. The dogs also knew that he was low; they were more active in their efforts to cheer him up, and sometimes more successful.

His mind impish and undisciplined even under these circumstances, Dan began to wonder if it could be proved that Cora Smith murdered Harry Curtis and Terence Barclay.

The problems were not moral but practical. Dan had recently tackled a practical problem of great complexity, and had finished up with a score of one hundred per cent and of zero. He wanted to do a bit better. He wanted to restore his self-esteem, regain Fiona's esteem, and save Sandra Hedges.

He began, despairingly, to construct a scenario quite as ludicrous as that built around Jim Gundry. He wove a fanciful, fantastic tapestry of what he would have liked to have happened, as though the nuns of Bayeux had rewritten history, as though the Normans had been defeated at Hastings except in the cloisters of that abbey, as though he were an official historian in *1984*, or a Marxist-Leninist, or a writer of political autobiography.

He had constructed a previous optimum account of events, but his chosen murderer had been murdered. He constructed a new optimum account. Thus:

Kittenish Cora Smith was indeed Harry Curtis's pet, his mascot, had been on and off for years. Her relationship with Harry went much further back than Sandra's. In fact they were married, years before, when Cora was very young. She had a bit of money then. Harry spent it, and consequently ditched her without ever forgetting her.

Harry met Sandra, who was ignorant and innocent and all the things Mrs Jenkyn said, and who had inherited a bit of money. Harry went through a form of marriage with Sandra, thus getting his hands on the money. What Sandra didn't know at the time, and still didn't know, was that that 'marriage' was worth less than the paper it was written on, the unfortunate bit of paper which had turned up in Nebraska and was sending her to prison. According to the laws of any country, Sandra was unmarried when she met Gordon Hedges. There was nothing wrong with her marriage to Gordon, or the status of the baby.

Sandra ran away from Harry, with what remained of her father's money. She ran all the way to Europe and to Salisbury and to a concert in the cathedral close.

Cora meanwhile had also 'married' again, an elderly man called Smith with a fair amount of money. He was old-fashioned and pig-headed, and he had never trusted a bank since the crash of 1929; consequently he kept his money in a sack under his mattress. Cora was his nurse, a private geriatric nurse hired by his family to keep him out of their way and off their consciences. They opposed the marriage, if they ever knew about it. They certainly opposed the will, when they heard about that. Perhaps they never did; perhaps there never was a will – simply a dead man on top of the mattress, and a sack of ten-dollar bills under it.

Harry Curtis heard about all this; naturally he would come to hear about any ex-wife of his who had come into a sackful of dollars. He found Cora and they joined up again. They did not have to marry, because they had been married all along. Cora was glad to have him back, because as far as she was capable of love it was Harry she loved. She had been and remained bitterly jealous of Sandra, bitterly jealous of being supplanted by Sandra even though it was only her money that made her so desirable. Cora was wiser this time: she made rules and conditions, and he made a lot of promises.

They saw the piece in the magazine. They read all about Gordon Hedges, including the part that said he had some money of his own. It was enough to get them to England, to Medwell Fratrorum. Cora, of course, staked Harry to the trip. She came along for the ride, out of curiosity, for fun, because she was paying, and in order to keep an eye on Harry. She was keeping an eye on her investment. She knew all about the whole thing from the start.

The airline tickets and the hotels used up much of what was left of Cora's 'husband's' money – Harry had already got through most of it. They needed the Hedges' money. Cora needed money, because without it she would lose Harry. He would never be anybody's property – she had to keep paying rent for him.

The door was part open between the bedrooms of the

Chestnut Horse, the light switched off in Cora's room, so that Harry Curtis could be sure that Terence Barclay didn't muck up his interview with Sandra, and so that, after Terence left, Cora could hear what was going on. Cora knew Harry well enough not to trust him. She knew that Sandra now had access to quite a lot of money, and that she was more beautiful than ever.

It was perfectly true that Cora had never seen the commando dagger in Harry's possession. She had seen it in her own possession. It was her dagger. She always had it with her, and she had it with her in that bedroom. The gun was hers, too.

She heard Sandra come, knowing who was coming and why. She expected one conversation and heard another. She heard Harry double-crossing her. She was as jealous and resentful of Sandra as ever. She heard Harry trying to arrange for Sandra to give him the money direct, cutting Cora out. She heard Harry saying that she, Sandra, had always been and would always remain his great love, that he was broken up when she left him, that what he wanted most was to have her back. He didn't care about Cora, never had, not really.

Probably he just about meant it when he said it. As with many heavily pregnant women, Sandra was in face truly more beautiful than ever. And a con-man does believe what he says, just while he says it. He couldn't be convincing if he didn't.

Harry hadn't forgotten that the door was open. He didn't care if Cora heard. That was the level of the man's awfulness – he didn't in the least mind lacerating Cora's feelings. He was done with her anyway, as he had just about spent all her money. He could still, and for a few more years, make money out of Cora, but he could make much more out of Sandra. Cora could hear about that just as well through a half-open bedroom door as any other way.

Sandra went away, having pleaded for time, needing time to get the money out of Gordon, who would need time to get it out of the bank.

Cora could kill two birds with one knife. She was a nurse – she knew enough anatomy to get a sharp point between ribs and beside the spine. She wiped her own fingerprints off the knife and put Harry's on it. She took all Harry's few papers and stuffed them in her handbag. She took her gun, in case she wanted to shoot anybody. It had Harry's fingerprints on the barrel because he had been cleaning and oiling it for her, or he had smuggled it through customs for her, or he had bought it for her in London, or she used his dead fingers for the prints. She went back into her room, and bolted the door between the rooms. She ran downstairs and out the back way, running after Sandra. She was going to blackmail Sandra into giving her an alibi. In the event she blackmailed Gordon into giving her exactly the same alibi.

She could blackmail them for a good deal more than that. No doubt she was going to, or had started. But once the police had evidence of the 'marriage' between Harry and Sandra in Nebraska, there was no longer anything to blackmail them about. Cora had to find another source of income, which was ready to hand from her very first evening in the village.

She thought she could blackmail Terence Barclay for as long as she wanted. But he turned out to have more power over her than she had over him. It turned out that he knew who had killed Harry.

How did he? How could he?

He was there a bit earlier, leaving and rejoining the party in the Church Rooms. Something was let drop. He saw that Cora had had all she could take of Harry Curtis. He heard threats. He heard Cora say that she would kill Harry if he took up with Sandra again, and he heard the brutality of Harry's answering laugh. On top of that, Terence must have got to know Cora pretty well, over their subsequent intimate weeks. When you have an affair with somebody you know if they're a murderer.

It was Cora he meant, when he said in the sealed letter that he knew who had killed Harry Curtis. Cora didn't know about that letter. All she knew was that he was holding over her head exposure as a murderess. Naturally she shot him in the back with her gun when a good opportunity presented itself – darkness, milling crowds, bustle and confusion, flashes and bangs of fireworks. She had been careful not to touch the gun without gloves or handkerchief in the meantime, and she still was. The gun had been bought illegally, and could not be traced to her unless it was found in her possession. She threw it in the long grass.

Dan examined this construction as he had examined that other one, looking for weaknesses and loose ends. He found none. The story had every merit. It deserved to be true.

Dan borrowed the typewriter in Sir George Simpson's study. Lady Simpson made him wash his hands before he used it; she looked as though she wanted him to wash his trousers too. She was amused but alarmed at the notion of Dan using a typewriter – she had, of course, heard about the paint in the Calloways' hall, and probably about the paint on Ted Goldingham's car.

While Dan washed his hands at the kitchen sink, Lady Simpson told him that the lovebirds were due back from Sicily any minute.

Dan said he wanted to type a letter to the surgeon about his mother's hip. Lady Simpson offered to compose and type the letter for him. Dan said his mother would have a fit if anybody else saw a letter to a surgeon about herself.

Dan had been well used to typewriters in his years at the bank. He used them for all sorts of purposes, including bank business. He only used two fingers, but he used them fast. He used them very slowly at the Simpsons', in order to spend the morning in that way rather than some other, and in order to retain his image for Lady Simpson.

He wrote to the Reverend Gordon Hedges, care of Admiral Jenkyn.

'You were seen putting the envelope into Admiral Jenkyn's letterbox,' said the Chief Detective Superintendent. 'The script matched Sir George Simpson's typewriter, which you had used. We have never liked anonymous letters, and we still don't, though I must say that in this case you did not take very great trouble to preserve your anonymity.'

'Nay,' said Dan, humbly torturing his tweed cap in fingers that writhed with bashfulness.

'What I require to know is not why you wrote that letter nor why you sent it anonymously. There were better ways of imparting the information, but I suppose the obvious, proper, conventional and legal methods would never appeal to, or even occur to, a tortuous and essentially antisocial personality such as yours. But I shall very nearly kill you unless I hear immediately *how you knew.*'

'Some o' 'at ben true?' said Dan, so astonished that the Super's car, and the Super himself, seemed to be revolving on a switchback.

'You know it's all true. *But how did you know?*'

'Which o' they bits ben true?'

'All o' they bits,' said the Super, in an angry parody of Dan's parody. *'How did you know?*'

'Ben nobbut wishful thinken,' said Dan.

They were waiting in the early evening near Amy Crate's cottage. The car had collected Dan from his own cottage, to his astonishment and his mother's frightened cackling. Dan was there not to be in at the death, but because of the Chief Superintendent's overpowering curiosity. With them were a Detective Sergeant and a uniformed policewoman. The Sergeant parked the car in the mouth of a lane near The Brambles. Amy Crate, raising her voice over the thunder of her television, told them that Mrs Smith was out and not expected back until late. A gentleman had come in a car. Most nights, gentlemen came in cars. It might be the same one or different ones. Amy Crate was not one to pry, and besides it was that programme about summat.

They guessed it would be a long wait, and it was. The Superintendent spent much of the time sizzling, like a pan of bubble-and-squeak on Dan's kitchen range.

The police in Nebraska had found evidence of the earlier marriage quite easily, as soon as they knew what to look for. Under one of his aliases, or perhaps under his real name, Harry Curtis had married Cora Lindstrom in front of a Justice of the Peace in 1975. There was no record of that marriage having been dissolved. The second marriages of both parties were bigamous and invalid. The marriage of the Reverend and Mrs Gordon Hedges was lawful and valid and would doubtless be permanent.

The Sergeant and the policewoman, taking pity on Dan, told him that everything he had invented was substantially true. Dan found that he was as incredulous as the Superintendent.

It was one in the morning when Cora Smith got back (or Cora Curtis, or whatever she properly was) and then she was ten minutes in the car in the dark with the gentleman. There was no need to bother or embarrass him. They waited for her in the garden. She broke down when she was cautioned and arrested; she was helped indoors by the policewoman to pack overnight things.

Dan found that he was expected to walk home.

Dan walked home slowly, much more tired than he usually was at two o'clock in the morning. He was exhausted not by physical labour, intellectual effort or emotional pressure, but by simple astonishment.

A complicated mystery had been solved (never mind why it was so complicated). He, Dan, had solved it. Not by peering at footprints, or smoking pipes, or punching at a computer, but by day-dreaming.

At other moments during the previous weeks, he had been in repeated danger of thinking things were true which he had invented. Now he was in danger of thinking that something must be fiction which was true.

He reached his cottage, dizzy with fatigue, and tried to quiet the dogs. He went to sleep at last with a thought buzzing round in his skull like a house-fly in a lampshade: would another fairy story he had written turn out to be true?

'How did you know about it?' said Fiona.

She was tanned from Sicily. She looked glorious. She took Dan by the shoulders and shook him, as though truth would come popping out of his throat like a fishbone.

Dan grinned. He knew it was a weak grin, not one of his good grins. Nobody could be made to believe that he had simply invented the story; he had nearly been arrested himself, for contempt of police, when he repeated that it was all wishful thinking.

Fiona let go of him, and stood looking at him furiously.

'The Super says you must have extrasensory perception,' she said. 'He thinks you're a warlock. I think he's right. It is true you splashed paint all over the Calloways' wallpaper? I think you were quite right, it's a horrid colour. I ought to have had a good time abroad, but I was missing . . . *How did you know?* Can't you say something? Can't you stop me talking too much? The Super says there never were so many idiotic distractions in a simple case, most of them caused by you. Of course it wasn't you that found that American watch, or saw the man with white hair in the headlights, but it *was* you who . . . The Super says it's the most irritating case they've ever had, almost all because of you . . . Sandra's gone back to the Jenkyns', did you know that? Gordon brought her back. The baby's due about tomorrow. The Bishop told Gordon he wouldn't accept his resignation. Nobody will. So he's unresigned. Did you miss me when I was away? Never mind about that. I missed . . . Never mind about that. I never saw anybody look so happy as Sandra Hedges. I saw her for a second. I'll never forget it. I wish you'd seen her. You will. They want to thank you. I think they want to make you a godfather for the baby, but I think that would be ridiculous. They'll be moving into the new Vicarage soon. The Jenkyns will be really sorry. I think the Calloways think you ought to offer to repaper their hall. Ted Goldingham thinks you ought to buy him a new car. I can't tell you what PC Gundry thinks . . . Everybody's been marrying me off to a man called Francis Morley. I don't suppose you've met him. He's really nice, but . . . I believe I *tried* to fall in love with him, but . . . My mother thinks you're some kind of spirit of the woods, something out of ancient folklore, she's terribly worried about me, she thinks I'll be bewitched and probably . . . You liked me laughing at you, didn't you? You tried to make me laugh and you succeeded. And then it got a bit too much. I went on and on laughing, and I don't think you ever guessed why. It was defence. Self-defence. I could see I was being suckered, kind of seduced, but as long as I kept laughing I was safe. I laughed and laughed, far more than I wanted to. I don't know why I thought I wanted to be safe. What I really wanted was . . . *Dan. Dan. Dan. Dan. Dan . . .*'